Ratio of Brookes
to Ashleys

WOL-VRIEY

Burning Bulb
PUBLISHING

Other Books By Wol-vriey:

The Bizarro Story of I
Meat Suitcase
Chainsaw Cop Corpse
Vegan Zombie Apocalypse
Boston Posh (Bud Malone #1)
Vegan Vampire Vaginas
Vagina Mundi
Melanie Nemesis Catchpole
Bizarro 101: A Basic Primer
Boston Corpse (Bud Malone #2)
Dr. Orgasm
Boston Lust (Bud Malone #3)
Pussy Transmission
Hell Dancer
Girls Are Not Smiling
Brainchew
Brainchew 2: Out of Their Heads
Blue Nightmares
Daria (An Erotic Nightmare)
Wet Bones
Mr. Ugly
Brutal
Evil
666
The Cleaverman
Perverse
The Virgin
The Book of Atrocities
The Final Girl
Women

Novellas and Short Stories By Wol-vriey

Big Trouble in Little Ass
Forever Ago Sunshine

Ratio of Brookes to Ashleys

WOL-VRIEY

Burning Bulb
PUBLISHING

Ratio of Brookes to Ashleys
By **Wol-vriey**

Burning Bulb Publishing
P.O. Box 4721
Bridgeport, WV 26330-4721
United States of America
www.BurningBulbPublishing.com

Cover designed by Gary Lee Vincent and Wol-vriey using a photo by Dima Valkov from Pexels.

First Edition.

Paperback Edition ISBN: 978-1-948278-45-4

Printed in the United States of America

PROLOGUE

The time was a few minutes to midnight on a warm midsummer Friday night.

The place was an ordinary apartment building in the slumbering little Massachusetts town of Raynham.

In that nondescript building, a young woman in her mid-twenties was busily making grim preparations in her living room.

The young woman didn't live alone, but she'd gotten out of going clubbing with the two friends she shared the apartment with by telling them she had a really bad headache and needed to stay home tonight.

Her friends had expressed their sympathy and then left to party with their boyfriends; one of them had just called home to inform her that neither of them would be back home till tomorrow afternoon at the earliest.

Perfect, just perfect, the young lady thought. It meant she had the whole apartment to herself till then. Much more than enough time for what she needed to do.

The young woman was a smallish blonde, and at the moment she was very depressed. But in this case, rather than her depression leeching her of purpose and energy, it galvanized her to get a move on.

First of all, she shut the windows of the living room and pulled the drapes closed over them. Her apartment was up on the third floor of the building, but there was another apartment house directly across the street and someone might look across from there to here and see what she was up to and call the police.

And besides that, she didn't want to take a chance on a gust of wind blowing out the black candles she'd just lit.

Once the drapes were shut, she turned off the apartment lights. Then she stripped off her tee shirt and panties, and now completely naked, sat cross-legged before the items she'd earlier arranged on the floor in the center of the living room, having moved aside the coffee table to free the area she now sat in.

The items on the floor all spoke of a morbid purpose. Most prominent of all was the wide cardboard rectangle, which she had cut from the packing box for the apartment's TV, and which she had afterwards flipped over on its brown unprinted side and decorated with a large black pentagram. Five black candles, lit and flickering, were arranged around the pentagram, one candle at each of its five points. Outside of the pentagram but still on the cardboard rectangle on its left, lay a very sharp knife, its blade gleaming brightly in the candlelight.

The two remaining objects on the floor in front of the seated young woman were the piece of paper placed in the center of the pentagram, and the cellphone she had placed on top of it. However, she had not placed the cellphone on the sheet of paper to keep it in place.

No, the cellphone was an important part of the ritual she was about to perform.

The cellphone—its screen kept permanently awake by an app—displayed the image of a young man of about her own age. He was passably handsome, with short brown hair, brown eyes and a calm smile. He looked like a very nice person.

She smirked at the thought. A nice person indeed! She'd thought he was nice too until he had . . .

The young woman sat there in front of the pentagram for a while, waiting till the clock on the wall to her left indicated that the hour was past midnight—the Witching Hour.

Then, heaving a loud sigh, she leaned forward and picked up her cellphone. She scowled at the image of the young man. Then she swiped the image sideways, revealing that it was half of a larger picture, the left half of which she occupied; she was grinning at the camera as she snapped the selfie of them together. Staring at it now, she found it hard to believe that she'd ever been that happy.

A sudden burst of pure rage filled her. "Time to do this," she whispered to herself in the candlelight.

That said, she swiped herself out of view again, so that the cellphone image was once more solely that of the young man.

Holding the cellphone in her left hand, with her right hand she now picked up the scrap of paper that it had covered. The paper had a spell written on it, one that she'd found on the internet after weeks of searching.

Then, frowning down at the young man she'd once been so happy with, she began reading the spell.

"Setirp st'se live eye mot emoc,
Th'gil esip sedtah tg norh t tse krads l'leh.
Th'gil pym noput saef d na emoc,
Efil eg durg y me vig d nahta edy m tae."

She felt a deep chill come over her as she pronounced the words, one that didn't end when she finished her recital of the spell and stuck the paper in the flame of one of the candles as the ritual required. As the paper burnt up she placed it into the middle of the pentagram and placed the cellphone right on top of it.

She smiled as the flames curled up around the cellphone and seemed to warp the boy's grinning image into a frowning one. The cellphone caught fire, but the flames burnt only around its edges, leaving its screen undamaged; and the cardboard that it rested on didn't burn at all.

Now that she'd recited the spell, she could already sense the darkness in her living room. The darkness—the evil she'd called up—was all around her, flickering like the candlelight—the darkness was hungry. It was hungry for blood; for her blood.

There was no going back now. She picked up the knife and then looked down at the image on the burning cellphone.

"I curse you, you jerk," she told the smiling picture. "By all the powers of Hell, I curse you to be forever as miserable in love as you have made me."

That said, she gripped the knife firmly in both hands and stabbed herself in the belly.

The pain hit her like . . . she had no words. She watched the blood jet out of her belly.

But strangely, at this moment her agony seemed inconsequential; what mattered to her was obtaining the result she desired; and to this end she felt the darkness in the room—whatever monstrous creature her spell had summoned from Hell's pits—strengthening her and guiding her hands to do what was necessary.

She pulled the knife from her belly and plunged it in again, deeper this time, till it almost touched her spine. Now the pain felt like monster jaws crunching down on her; she was a chunk of meat being chewed. More blood flooded out. Her hands and forearms had turned a glistening crimson, and her crotch was a lake with a border of blonde trees.

Now she raked the razor-sharp blade sideways and sliced herself wide open.

And then, gasping in pain and shivering in fright from the fear of her inevitable death, she yanked her bleeding intestines out of her belly and dropped them on top of her burning cellphone with its grinning image of the man she hated most in all the world.

Smothered by dripping flesh, the flames instantly went out.

Her death came very quickly after that. But she died happy.

The deed was done. She imagined she heard the darkness she'd summoned giggling in delight at her sacrificial offering.

CHAPTER 1

Dead? Ashley Cummins dead?

As he pulled his blue Ford pickup truck over by the driveway of his house on Raynham's Britton Street and parked, Mike Broadman once more tried to get his mind around the shocking news.

She's frigging dead? But . . . but . . . ?

Ashley Cummins had died last night. She'd committed suicide. The way the cops had described her death, she'd offed herself like she was practicing hara-kiri 101. All that had been missing to simulate that tableau of Japanese ritual suicide was someone chopping off her head after she'd disemboweled herself.

Ugh! Just the thought of that made Mike nauseous. Feeling unable to leave the pickup truck just yet, he leaned his head forward on the steering wheel and let the bad feelings wash over him.

And disemboweling herself wasn't the worse of it: Ashley had apparently killed herself over a photograph of himself. The cops had found her partially torched cellphone with his image frozen on its screen.

Thankfully, it had clearly been suicide—Mike was in no trouble with the law over her death. But a lady detective—a Shania Banks— had visited him at work to inform him of Ashley's death and enquire about their past relationship.

Detective Banks had also said something about Ashley performing a devilish ritual at the time of her suicide, but Mike had already zoned out by then. He'd merely 'ummed' along with her morbid monologue.

She killed herself to a photograph of me?

This knowledge made Mike feel even sicker. Talk about leaving a legacy of guilt behind oneself and pointing a blaming finger.

Mike Broadman had broken up with Ashley Cummins a month ago and had tried to forget her. But now it appeared he'd never be able to do so.

They had dated for two months. He'd initially liked her a lot; they'd laughed and loved and done all the sweet things new couples did. But Ashley had suffered from terrible mood swings—one moment she'd be happier than a clown and the next moment she'd be sadder than a convict on death row, and in both cases without any apparent external triggers.

After a while Mike had decided she was simply too dangerous to be with; he'd also hated the feeling of uncertainty that surrounded her.

When Mike had told Ashley that he wouldn't be seeing her anymore, she'd acted calmly enough. She'd smiled and told him it was okay; that she didn't think their relationship was working out either. And that had seemed to be that.

They'd spoken on the phone a few times since then, and Ashley had even congratulated Mike when he'd informed her he'd begun dating Jane Fowler, a girl she'd attended high school with. That conversation—a week ago—had been the last time they'd spoken to each other.

And now . . .

Why'd you do it, Ash? Even I don't think I'm worth you losing your life over.

Mike sighed and leaned back up in the car, placing his head on the headrest though keeping his eyes shut. There were tears in his eyes; he palmed them away.

Across the street a trio of chattering teenage girls dressed in faded denim walked past. One of them was walking a dog wearing a red collar. Cars passed him back and forth but he hardly sensed their presence. For the moment, the world seemed frozen. In Mike's soul this pleasant Saturday afternoon had turned grim.

He did his best not to feel guilty about Ashley's death, but the evidence spoke for itself; it was a psychic attorney relentlessly prosecuting him.

Ash made it as clear as daylight why she was killing herself. And what the hell was the detective saying about devil worship or whatever?

Mike finally felt recovered enough to get out of his pickup truck. He'd been working the afternoon shift today; but once the police detective had left him, there was no way he'd been able to continue. He'd just stood staring into space in the electronics section of the Cashstretch supermarket, while the customers had in turn stared at him, as if hoping he wasn't about to go psycho and run amuck shooting everyone.

Finally the store's assistant manager had called him into her office and asked him what the matter was. She was a sympathetic woman, and once Mike told her what had happened, she'd let him take the rest of the afternoon off. Someone else would cover for him.

Mike walked around the hood of the pickup truck and stepped over the curb up onto his driveway. But then, feeling that something was a little peculiar, he paused and looked back to where he'd parked the truck. He shook his head, realizing that he'd been so distracted by the bad news about Ashley that he'd parked out in the street, as if he planned on merely picking up something from the house and didn't want the hassle of having to reverse back out into the street. He considered getting back into the truck and driving it properly into the yard, but then decided 'fuck it.' Repositioning the vehicle wasn't any kind of a priority.

He looked at his watch; the time was four-fifteen. He sighed. All he had in mind to do now was to get himself a few cold beers from the fridge and drink them, then lie in bed until Jane came over at eight. They were supposed to go out with friends, but now Mike wasn't in the mood to party. He hoped Jane would understand his reasons for cancelling though. Though much more emotionally stable than the late Ashley Cummins, Mike hoped his new girlfriend wouldn't interpret his current depression as him still carrying a torch for the dead girl. Her doing so would completely crash this already nosedived day.

He plodded up the driveway to the house, dully noting that Kirk's silver Nissan Altima sedan was parked in the garage.

Kirk Coombs was one of the two friends that Mike shared the old bungalow with. But Kirk really lived with his father (over on the east side of town) and only used the house as a pad to bring girls to. Seeing Kirk's car in the garage on Saturday afternoon meant he had a young woman in the house.

Mike's other housemate was his bestie Bob Evans. Mike figured Bob would be home now, which would give him a sympathetic ear to talk to. Then he remembered that Bob had texted him at work (just before the detective arrived) saying that he was going to pick up something from a friend's place.

Mike shrugged. He reached the house, climbed the front porch and halted for a few seconds with his key poised to slot into the lock. Knowing that Kirk had a girl in the house, he wasn't certain he really wanted to enter it. Kirk and the young woman were certain to be making a hell of a racket in Kirk's bedroom, and noise was one thing Mike wasn't up to coping with at the moment.

But neither did Mike feel in the mood to drive out again. He just wanted to get a little drunk and try to forget about Ashley Cummins's suicide. Forgetting, however, was certain to be hard to do: Detective Banks's description of the death scene had been very graphic, with Mike afterwards wondering if she'd gone into such detail about the suicide because she also blamed him for Ashley's death and wanted him to feel as guilty as possible.

Mike hovered in indecision, but finally decided that the house seemed silent enough.

Maybe Kirk and the chick are done balling and have fallen asleep, and I can grab myself a beer and . . .

He opened the door and stepped inside. Yes, Kirk definitely had a lady friend over; a feminine perfume lingered in the living room. Mike also imagined for a moment that he heard slurping noises quite nearby.

Despite his gloom, he allowed himself a moment to admire Kirk's facility with women. Though the guy was a close friend, Mike would be the first to admit that Kirk was a loser; he couldn't hold down a job to save his life and spent whatever he did earn drinking; the silver Altima parked outside really belonged to his father. But where women were concerned, it was a different matter entirely. With women, it appeared that Kirk couldn't lose—good or bad, rich or penniless, they all loved him. For him, seducing the fair sex seemed easier than breathing. Often, Kirk could get a young lady into his bed mere hours after meeting her. And that went for girls Kirk met in the daytime too, not just in bars or at parties at night.

So Kirk Coombs was the kind of sleazebag that women always claimed they hated, but then sneaked off to sleep with behind their respectable boyfriend's back.

And it was while enviously considering this last fact that Mike realized that he recognized the female purse that lay on the couch.

Hey, that's the purse Jane bought last week at the mall! Oh no, not her too . . . no, she can't be. . . . No, that sonofabitch Kirk can't be . . . !

Mike felt cold. Suddenly forgetting all about Ashley Cummins, he quietly made his way further into the living room, and then through it. He let his ears locate Kirk and his sexual partner.

There was no moaning or gasping, just that slurping sound; and when Mike stepped into the dining room area, he understood why. Kirk was seated on a chair with his fly open and was drinking from a can of beer, while Jane—Mike's new girlfriend Jane—was down on her knees fellating him. Jane was still fully clothed, in sneakers, denim pants and a white top. Her red lips were a rising and falling strawberry ring around Kirk's erection.

Her long black hair was in her eyes, so that she at first didn't notice Mike.

Kirk did though. He was so surprised to see Mike that he dropped his beer. The beer then emptied over Jane's head and wet her top, which in turn made her pull her mouth off of Kirk's penis and look at him in surprise.

"What did you do that for?" she asked. Then, seeing that Kirk was looking past her, she turned around and saw Mike.

She rolled her eyes on seeing Mike. "Oh, it's you." And then to Mike's total surprise, she once more dipped her mouth back down on Kirk's penis and resumed sucking on it as if he wasn't there.

Kirk at first looked apologetically at Mike, but then Jane pulled her mouth off of his penis again and stared coldly at him. "Hey, baby, you're getting soft! Stop thinking about this loser!"

"But . . . but . . . but . . . !" Mike sputtered, none of this making sense. "But . . . Jane, you're my girlfriend!" It seemed dumb to have to state the obvious in a case like this, where the girlfriend in question was down on her knees, with another man's penis in her mouth.

"Sorry, man, it just happened," Kirk said, raising his hands in a pacifying gesture, and then running the fingers of both hands back through his dark hair like he was combing it. "I mean, you know how it is . . ." But even while he was apologizing, Mike could see the smirk that Kirk was trying to hide; the smirk on his handsome face that proclaimed, *I'm sexier than you, you loser!*

Mike expected to feel enraged, but no rage came. As he understood these things, this was exactly the kind of situation that made one run into the kitchen and grab a knife and stab both of these betrayers to death. He tried to summon up an image of himself stabbing Kirk and Jane multiple times, while blood squirted from their wounds and sprayed all over the walls, but it was a futile attempt; the image fizzled out as if it sensed his apathy. He felt no rage, only a sad resignation; an acceptance that he and Jane's relationship had inexplicably failed.

And then he understood why he was so accepting of this situation: the news of Ashley's horrible death had worn him out. Nothing was worse than death.

There in the dining room, time stretched out awkwardly for the three of them. Despite Jane's best efforts to re-erect it, Kirk's penis had now completely wilted.

"Hey, Kirk, I've got a great idea," Jane said suddenly. She leapt to her feet and pulled Kirk up after her, then she shot Mike a black look. "Let's go into the bedroom where this loser can't watch us."

She walked off, dragging Kirk after her. She had a good figure and a very tight ass, and it hurt Mike to watch her walk off like that, knowing she wasn't his girlfriend anymore. But really he felt more numbed than sad.

Once they'd left (and Jane had pointedly slammed the door to Kirk's bedroom) Mike walked into the kitchen and got his beer. He still felt dazed. He sucked at the beer for half a minute or so, and then once the can was empty, he ditched it in the trash and walked out of the kitchen. From the loud noises erupting from the hallway—"Yes, yes, fuck my ass, man! Fuck it like that!"—Jane had clearly gotten Kirk hard again.

No way in hell am I gonna sit around listening to those two idiots, Mike decided.

He left the house and walked to the foot of the driveway. For a few seconds he toyed with the idea of driving his pickup truck, then he decided against it. In his current frame of mind there was a very high likelihood of him killing either himself or someone else with the vehicle.

He set off walking for Ruby's Truck Stop. Maybe the walk would help him clear his head.

When he reached the Broadway intersection he got out his cellphone and tapped off a quick text to Bob, asking Bob to meet him at Rudy's.

CHAPTER 2

At Rudy's Truck Stop, Mike slid into a booth near the bar and signaled to a waitress.

The time being late afternoon, Rudy's wasn't yet full of people, but there were enough fellow drinkers present that Mike could feel anonymous, just another random sufferer sailing on life's ailing sea.

The waitress came over to take his order. Mike was too wrapped up in his thoughts to note anything about her other than her perfume, and that only because he found that its pleasant smell distracted from his misery. He ordered a beer and she walked off again. Once she'd left, the regular smells of the place—sweat and spilled beer and the ever present aroma of fried food—returned to keep him company.

The beer arrived and he drank. The jukebox was playing something by Slain Jane:

"Shut up and do me, baby.
Stop talking and eat my . . . ughh!
Yeah, lick me like you really love me . . . !"

Mike tuned Jane O and the boys out.
Shit! I can't believe this is happening to me . . .
The walk up here hadn't really cleared Mike's mind. He still felt lost in a haze, with death and betrayal stalking him, men and women in long cloaks and clutching long daggers lurking in the shadows.

At a point he lifted his beer bottle to his lips and found it was empty. He signaled to the same waitress for another one. She nodded back, but he had to wait because the joint's proprietor Rudy—a shaggy brute of a man—was handing her a tray of drinks for some customers over on the other side of the room.

Someone opened the front door then, letting in the noises of the adjacent highways, both from overhead and here below, seeing as the truck stop stood beside the I-495 overpass over Route 138.

Mike's second beer arrived. A bit less sad now, he paid more attention to the waitress. She was young and attractive, with long dark hair. She was new; she'd not been working here the last time he'd visited.

"Are you okay?" she asked as she set down his beer.

"I've had better days," Mike replied her. "This is one of those days you wish you could sleep through . . . and wake up a month later."

Her eyes narrowed. "That bad?"

Mike laughed bitterly. "If today got any worse, I'd be in a funeral home. At the moment the only reason I'm still alive is that I don't own a gun."

She looked alarmed. "Oh, that's really horri—"

"Hey, dude, sorry I'm late," a male voice interrupted, then added. "Hey, Linda, how's it going?"

Mike and the waitress both looked at the speaker. It was his bestie Bob Evans.

Mike wasn't surprised that Bob knew the girl. Bob was a very social guy and seemed to know everyone in town, which, considering that the entire population of Raynham barely ticked fifteen thousand, might not be considered a huge achievement, but Mike hardly knew all their neighbors.

Linda smiled at Bob and then pointed worriedly at Mike. "Your friend here was just talking about killing himself," she whispered to Bob as he seated himself opposite Mike.

"Oh, don't worry, I'll be fine," Mike said. "And let's have some beer for Bobby too please."

"Yeah, sure," she said. "Hey, do you guys want something to eat too?"

Mike shook his head. "No food for me. I'm just drinking."

She looked at Bob, who also shook his head. "Maybe a burger, but later."

Linda hurried off back to the bar, where Rudy was already waiting impatiently with another customer's order. The other waitress was stepping out from the diner kitchen with two trays of fries and burgers.

Bob Evans was twenty-seven, the same age as Mike, a lanky and pale-haired young man. He worked at the Walmart Supercenter down on Broadway. Bob was a very laid-back fellow, and was extremely loyal and reliable too; in short, the sort of guy that you were glad was your best friend.

"What the hell is going on?" Bob asked Mike. "Dude, I stopped off at home before coming here and . . . well, I don't know how else to put this, so . . . when I got to our house, Kirk was moving out."

Mike frowned. "Moving out?"

Bob nodded. "Yeah, dude. He was loading all his stuff into his dad's car and . . . what's even crazier was that Jane was helping him carry his stuff out of the house and the two of them were kissing like they'd just gotten married. Once she even grabbed his package through his pants."

Bob stopped talking and looked at Mike, his eyes demanding answers. Mike lifted his beer to his lips and took a long pull. But once again, he realized that the bottle was empty. He wondered if the bottles had been half-full to begin with.

Thankfully, Linda returned just then with Bob's beer. Mike snatched the beer up immediately she set it down in front of Bob and then grinned at the surprised young woman. "Another beer for my friend, sugar."

She scowled at him and whispered, "Hey, man, my name ain't 'sugar,' it's Linda."

He grinned back. "Yeah, I know it's Linda, but you look really sweet. Can I call you 'candy' or 'honey' instead?"

She mused on that, suppressing a grin. "At least you're not speaking of killing yourself now," she finally said, and then added: "Hey, Rudy doesn't like me chatting with the customers—he thinks I'm flirting."

"Hey, sugar, don't forget Bob's beer," Mike called after her as he hurried off again.

Then he took a long gulp of the filched beer and sighed at Bob. "I dunno what just came over me, talking to her like that. I think it's 'cos she's the best thing that's happened to me all day."

Bob stared at him in complete incomprehension. "Are you saying that you and Jane just broke up? She's with Kirk now?"

Mike laughed. Suddenly, life seemed to him to be a total comedy. Well, *his* life anyway. "I wish that was all that happened."

And then he told Bob all about Ashley Cummins's suicide and Jane's subsequent betrayal.

Bob listened in shock and gawped at Mike.

"What the hell is wrong with you two?" Linda said when she returned with Bob's beer.

"Huh?" Bob asked, turning to stare at her.

"Bobby," Linda whispered patiently while setting the beer in front of him, "at the moment you look worse than your friend did when he arrived." She gave Mike a studying glance. "Now, in fact, he looks better than you do. What is the matter with both of you?"

Mike shrugged. "You really wanna know, sugar?"

"Hey, I've already told you to stop calling me 'sugar!' But what the heck, yeah, I really wanna know what's bugging you both."

Mike smiled. "Okay, have dinner with both of us and we'll tell you."

Linda looked surprised by the request. She looked from Mike to Bob and apparently decided the pair were harmless enough, because she replied: "Okay, okay. I get off in"—she glanced up at the clock behind the bar—"an hour and fifteen minutes. So you'll have to wait."

Mike nodded. "Sugar, I've nowhere I wanna go. I'd rather be here with you."

She almost blushed. "Hey, stop that! I ain't your sugar."

"Not yet, you're not. You got a boyfriend?"

"No. What's that got to do with anything?"

Mike smiled. "That's great, 'cos I'm single too." He pointed to Bob. "You can ask Bobby how single I am."

Linda stared inquiringly at Bob, who had his beer to his lips.

Bob lowered his beer and nodded back. "Yeah, at the moment Mike is the most single dude in Massachusetts. He'd fetch top dollar at an 'unattached dude' auction." Then he sighed. "Hey, Linda, you'd better get back to the bar. Rudy's staring knives at your back."

"Oh, shit, you guys are gonna lose me my job." She turned and hurried off again.

"She's cute," Mike said. "I just hope she's not a slut like Jane."

"Oh, Linda's a really nice girl," Bob said. Then he sighed. "But then again, I really thought Jane was a nice girl too."

***

When, two hours later, Mike related to Linda Dunning what had happened to put him in an emotional funk, all she could do was gape at him too.

CHAPTER 3

Time does heal all wounds.

It was now two weeks later and Mike had almost forgotten about Jane's betrayal.

Once she'd been certain he wasn't a suicidal drunk but a sensible, well-adjusted young man, Linda had happily agreed to date Mike. And Bob had been right—she was a very nice girl. Mike would be the first to admit that he was obviously on the rebound and their relationship had begun rather fast for him, but he found it much better being with Linda than being alone.

She made him very happy and he could tell that he made her happy too.

It was Friday night. Mike and Bob had just picked up Linda from work and were cruising along Route 123, heading toward Attleboro, where Kimchi Chocolate Stereo were playing tonight. Mike had had the concert tickets for a month now with Jane as his original planned date for tonight. Jane loved KCS.

Mike hadn't heard from Jane since that fateful Saturday afternoon, and he hadn't seen Kirk either. He was glad on both counts. He'd run into Kirk's younger brother Eddie at work a few days ago, but he'd been too busy to chat.

Mike was driving the pickup truck, with Linda riding shotgun. Bob was in the back, playing *Mafia vs Zombies* on his cellphone.

"You know, baby, I've been thinking," Linda said.

"About what?" Mike asked, not looking at her because they'd just entered Attleboro and he was turning off the highway. The concert didn't start until nine; the three of them planned to have dinner and drinks somewhere else first.

"It's about my job at Rudy's," Linda went on. "I'm thinking of quitting and looking for another one. I can't shake the feeling that Rudy don't like me for some reason."

Still keeping his focus on the road, Mike nodded. They'd discussed this before. Linda was a laid-back character, while, though not a mean sonofabitch, Rudy was an aggressive kind of guy. The upshot of this was that Rudy didn't think that Linda (who *was* dedicated to her job and was working as hard as she could) was giving her best to his business.

"Hahaha!" Bob laughed from the backseat. "The old guy's just scared Mike's gonna steal you from him."

"Yeah, I agree," Mike said. "And when I do, he'll ban me from drinking at his place for life."

They were approaching a crossroads. The traffic lights were green and Mike sped up a little to make the crossing before they turned red.

"I hear you both, but I still think it's more than that," Linda said. She'd gotten her compact out of her purse and was checking out her makeup. "He's always acting like I'm rubbing him the wrong—Yeow! Careful, Mike!"

Mike had stomped on the brakes, because ahead of them a driver in the intersecting lane had run the stoplight. He got the pickup truck stopped just in time; the crossing car scraped against the front bumper, but then . . .

Bang! The pickup truck was rammed by the vehicle behind them which hadn't been able to stop in time.

What happened next?

Mike wasn't wearing a seatbelt; Linda was. But while Mike was merely bumped forward into the steering wheel and Bob was flung forward into the rear of Mike's seat, Linda went flying forward out through the windshield.

At that moment time almost seemed to slow down. Mike distinctly heard Linda's seatbelt snap. He saw her body leave her seat; saw her head strike the windshield and punch a hole through it, while the glass turned into a fractured spider web; and then, worst of all, as the pickup truck jerked up and down from the impact, he saw her body twist in a weird way that pulled her neck sideways through the shattered glass.

One moment Linda had a head, the next she didn't. The truck stopped jerking up and down and Linda's headless body fell backwards into the passenger seat, squirting blood everywhere.

Mike stared in speechless horror at the corpse next to him. Then tears filled his eyes, and he reached out a hand and grabbed her lifeless arm.

"Oh, Linda, noooooo!"

"What the hell happened, dude? Why'd you stop like that?"

Bob, who was stunned and had no idea what had just happened, looked forward between the seats. He saw Linda's headless body, exclaimed, "Shit, dude!" and then slumped back onto the backseat and looked as horrified as Mike did.

"Nooooo!" Mike kept moaning.

The paramedics found all three of them in the car like that.

CHAPTER 4

For two weeks after Linda's funeral, Mike somehow achieved the miracle of not slipping into full-blown depression. A sudden increase in his responsibilities at work had helped with this, as the additional workload meant he was mentally preoccupied for most of the day.

But when he got home, he was all alone. Bob worked as an overnight stocker at Walmart. Most workdays, Bob was preparing to leave the house when Mike got in from work. And then Mike would be left alone with the ghastly memory of how Linda had died.

What perplexed him the most about her death was the sheer improbability of what had happened.

Mike thought it conceivable that given the right/wrong conditions a seatbelt could snap. But that definitely wouldn't be when you got bumped from behind by a car that wasn't speeding. And a bump like that shouldn't have pitched Linda forward through the windshield either. Even the accident specialists couldn't explain how Linda had lost her head.

He'd since replaced the shattered windshield of his pickup truck, but each time he climbed into the vehicle the accident replayed through his mind and a dense sadness welled up in him.

It was a classic tragicomedy. The guy who'd run the red light and caused the accident hadn't been either a road-rager or a drunk, but was a panic-stricken first time dad-to-be who was rushing his pregnant wife to hospital after she'd unexpectedly gone into early labor. The police still had no idea what to do with the guy.

Mike spent most evenings drinking himself into a stupor. He knew it wasn't good for him, but what else was there to do? It was either that or run himself crazy with recriminations: *If only we hadn't gone to the concert . . . if only we'd stayed home . . . if only Linda had been sitting in the back . . . if only . . . if only . . .*

Mike didn't miss the oddity that two women he'd been in relationships with had died in two weeks; both of them in conditions of extreme violence. Of course this was just a sad coincidence, but still, the overhanging specter of Ashley's suicide made Linda's death seem that much more unnatural.

Thankfully, the police—meaning, in this case Detective Shania Banks again—were once more convinced there hadn't been any foul play on Mike's part. Had Bob not been riding with them that night, there might have been suspicion that Mike had beheaded Linda beforehand and was driving her corpse somewhere to dispose of it.

Not everyone was so lenient in their views, however. It appeared that Mike Broadman would be persona non grata at Rudy's Truck Stop for a long while to come.

Even Kirk had checked up on Mike. He didn't come to the house, but he'd vid-called via WhatsApp and told Mike he was really sorry to hear about Linda, and was equally sorry about what had happened between he and Jane, and that if Mike needed a friend to talk to he was just a phone call away.

"Or you can just come round to the house," he'd finished with a grin. "Dad's constantly asking after you."

Yeah right, Mike had thought. *So you can steal my next girlfriend too?*

He'd quickly realized that while speaking to him, Kirk was doing his best to keep a straight face. His initial thought was that Kirk was trying not to smirk at him, but this turned out to be wrong, because Kirk's eyes had suddenly rolled up in his head and the cellphone's area of focus had lowered slightly, letting Mike see the female head bobbing up and down in his lap. The sonofabitch had been getting a blowjob—possibly from Jane—while expressing his sympathies over Mike's bad luck!

Dammit! Enraged, Mike had cut the video call and poured himself some whiskey.

***

"Hey, dude, gotta talk to you about something important," Bob said at breakfast that Sunday morning.

"I'm not in the mood, dude," Mike said, scooping sugar onto his Cheerios. "And can't it wait till you properly wake up? As it is you look dead on your feet."

It was almost 9 a.m. in the morning. As was usual, Bob had gotten in from night-stocking Walmart two hours ago and gone straight to his room. But now, standing here in their dining room in his dirty white shorts and with his hair scattered, he looked like he hadn't slept in the interim.

"No, this is very important," Bob retorted. He brushed blonde hair out of his eyes, fetched himself a cereal bowl from the kitchen and pulled up a chair to the dining table.

"This is *very* important," he repeated, while pouring cereal into his bowl. "Very, very important."

"What is?" Mike asked. He wasn't interested. The best thing about Sundays was that you could drink all day and mope about lost loves . . . But it looked like Bob had other plans in mind.

"It's about the current state of your love life," Bob said sagely while adding milk to his breakfast.

"Aw, come on, man," Mike said, suddenly losing all interest in his own Cheerios. He lay down his spoon on the table and stared coldly across it at Bob. "Gimme a break. We've already been over this. Right now, I *don't have* a love life. My last three attempts at dating women have all been disasters. At the moment, I'm scared to even smile at a girl in case she likes me. It's almost like I'm cursed or something."

"Exactly," Bob agreed. "And someone else thinks so too."

"Huh? What the hell are you talking about? Someone else what?"

Bob ate some cereal before replying. "Well, dude, I mentioned your troubles to a friend of mine at work—a dude named Dave."

"Aw, man, what you do that for? You didn't tell him my name, did you?"

Bob shook his head. "No, no, I didn't let on that it was you. I just told Dave that a guy I knew had been having major woman issues—like continual . . . recurring bad luck girl issues and I described them to him. Told him one girl committed suicide, the next one cheated on you, and the third . . . well, I said a serial killer got her . . . and then I added that it all happened within the space of a fortnight."

"So . . . ? And . . . ?"

Bob shrugged. "Immediately I'd finished, Dave looked at me and said my friend was hexed."

"Hexed?"

"Dude, you know . . . witchcraft . . . a bad luck spell. Hey, and once Dave said that, I immediately remembered what the cops said about Ashley Cummins performing a black magic ritual over your picture on her cellphone."

Mike had thought of that too. The idea that the late Ashley Cummins might have placed a bad luck spell on him had occurred to him too. But he'd so far managed to disregard it.

"Listen, what happened with Ashley and Linda was just a sequence of nasty coincidences," he told Bob slowly, his breakfast cereal now soggy and totally forgotten. "Let's not travel to dumbass-ville with all this magic crap. I don't believe in ghosts."

Bob shrugged. "I do. And Ashley Cummins certainly did." He ate some more cereal before continuing. "Anyway, Dave doesn't believe in magic either—"

"But you just said . . ."

"No, he doesn't, but he knows the symptoms of a hex, see, because his old man's into paranormal stuff in a big way."

Mike stared curiously at Bob. "His dad?"

Bob pushed his cereal bowl away too. "Yeah, yeah, dude. Apparently Dave's dad Master Slim is some kinda paranormal consultant. The cops consult him when they're trying to find missing kids and stuff like that. Hold on a minute and I'll get his card for you."

Before Mike could protest, Bob had left the dining room. Mike sat there, refusing to accept what he was hearing. *Master Slim? And no, I am not under any kind of a hex—I am not being dogged by a magic spell.*

Bob soon returned. He handed Mike a black business card with white lettering amidst a background of red occult symbols. 'Master Slim: grandmaster of occult practices,' the card read.

Mike looked enquiringly at Bob. "grandmaster of occult practices? Are you frigging serious?"

"According to Dave, the old guy casts the occasional spell too," Bob said. "He suggests that you go consult him. Not too expensive— just a hundred bucks."

"No, I won't go and see him," Mike said firmly, waving the ornate business card in the air. "And I'll tell you why, dude."

Bob looked thoughtful. "Why? I'm listening."

In the short interim while Bob had left their dining room, Mike had thought of a very simple counterargument to all of this 'hex' and 'bad luck spell' nonsense.

"Okay, reason along with me," he said. "Yes, I've had three bad . . . no, sad . . . no, three *disastrous-ending* . . . relationships one after the other. Okay, so for the sake of argument, let's agree that I am being haunted by a spell cast by Ashley Cummins . . ."

"Go on."

". . . Yeah, and that that spell killed Linda . . ."

"Yeah?"

". . . So, what about Jane? Jane—that nasty slut—is still alive and well and is possibly sucking Kirk's dick as we speak." Mike smirked at Bob. "So, you see, *dude*, there's no logic to it. Not unless you want to tell me that Ashley's spell also made Jane cheat on me."

He shot Bob a pointed stare while saying this, as if daring him to contradict him.

Bob shrugged. "Ah, you got me there, dude. Nah, I don't think that's what happened at all. That was just Kirk doing his old trick of wowing the ladies—we've seen that happen too many times to ascribe it to magic." Then he yawned. "Aw shit, I gotta get back to bed; see ya later."

Bob gathered up both of their cereal bowls and carried them into the kitchen, then he staggered off down the hallway to his bedroom.

Once Bob was gone, Mike dropped Master Slim's business card and let it flutter down onto the table. Then he got himself a beer, and smiling coolly, he walked into the living room and turned on the TV.

Sunday isn't ruined after all, he thought as he flipped through the sports channels. *I can still get a little drinking done today.*

It however turned out that he was wrong.

***

Mike had barely begun drinking—he was on his second beer—when his cellphone rang. He picked it up, glanced at the screen and winced. It was Jane calling.

"What the hell does the slut want?" he growled. He wasn't about speaking to her, that was for sure. She'd not called or texted him since the day he'd caught she and Kirk screwing, and he'd been relieved about that.

He ignored the phone and waited for it to stop ringing. But then it instantly started up again. He ignored it again and the same thing happened. He considered throwing the phone at the TV or out through the window, but finally realized that unless he turned it off, his ex-girlfriend would keep calling him till he picked it up.

So he picked it up. "Yeah, what the hell do you want?"

"Mike? Oh, thanks, thanks so much for answering!"

That threw Mike. He'd been expecting her to swear at him or something. He'd thought that maybe she was just phoning to tell him she'd forgotten something at his house that she planned on coming over to pick up. But no, she sounded genuinely pleased that he'd answered the phone.

"Jane, what do you want? Why are you calling me? Listen, I'm busy at the moment and I can't—"

"Just listen, Mike, please," she breathlessly interrupted him. "I need to talk to you about something."

"We've nothing to discuss. You made that very clear to me. Don't worry, I got the message loud and clear."

There was silence on the other end of the line. Then Jane said, "Listen, I'm sorry for what happened between us."

"You're sorry? Jane, what's this all about?"

"Just listen, please? First of all, I'm sorry about what happened to Linda. It was really horrible and I can't even begin to imagine how you're feeling right now. I really can't."

"That's nice of you. Thanks for your condolences. And now, if you don't mind, I'd like to carry on drowning my misery in beer. Goodbye—"

"No, don't hang up on me! Linda's death isn't the primary reason I called. I *really* need to talk to you. If you hang up, I'm going to have to come over to the house to see you."

No, Mike didn't want her coming over here. Better to listen to Jane on the phone than see her in person; he didn't feel like looking at the dirty mouth she'd wrapped around Kirk's penis. But . . . but . . . what the . . . ? Was Jane crying now? Yes, she was. She was sobbing loud and clear over the line.

Oh, poor slut. Maybe Kirk just broke up with her.

"Okay, I'm listening," he said coldly. "But make it quick. Like I said, I plan to spend today getting drunk and mourning."

"Thanks for listening to me," she said quickly, her words tumbling out between her sobs. "Listen, just hear me out, okay. This might not mean anything to you, but it's important to me to get it off of my chest."

"I'm listening, Jane, I'm listening." He took a sip of beer and prayed she'd hurry up with whatever she had to confess and that it wouldn't take too long.

Confess? Maybe she'd mistaken his house for the Catholic church across town. Or maybe she wanted to reveal that she'd previously slept with Kirk's brother Eddie too. Maybe what she needed to get off her chest were stubbornly adhesive smears of Kirk's semen and she wanted Mike's advice on a suitable skin cleanser. Who knew what the hell the slut wanted?

"Okay, now," Jane began, "even though I know that there's no way you'll ever accept me back, I'm really sorry about everything."

"You already told me that. That's fine; and yes, there's no way ever that I'm gonna take you back." He sighed. "Jane, I caught you sucking Kirk's dick!"

She sobbed loudly then and oddly, he found himself feeling sorry for her.

"I know, Mike, I know!" she wailed miserably. "And that's the problem! I still have no idea why I cheated on you. I was truly in love with you and yet on that Saturday afternoon I felt a sudden compulsion to have sex with Kirk. Kirk and I were just sitting in the living room chatting and then all of a sudden . . . it felt like I was under a spell, one that I was powerless to resist . . ."

Mike had been taking a fresh gulp of beer, but now he almost choked on it. The beer sputtered from his lips and sprayed over the rug. He recalled his recent conversation with Bob and felt thrills of dread shoot up and down his spine.

"Mike, are you still there? Are you listening to me? I really need you to understand this."

"Yeah, go on," Mike said, his voice no longer hard and brittle, but worried. "What do you mean—you felt like you were under a spell?"

"That's what it seemed like to me—like a wind or a haze had suddenly filled my brain, and I couldn't resist what it demanded of me. All of a sudden, I felt like I had to get even with you for some reason, even though I had no idea what that reason was. Doing the wrong thing seemed so right at the time . . . All of a sudden—completely out of the blue—it seemed very important to me to hurt you, to *really* hurt you. Mike, are you listening?" Jane was really, really weeping now.

"I'm listening."

"I even let Kirk fuck me in the ass."

"Yeah, yeah, I heard you encouraging him to do so. You seemed to be really enjoying it. You didn't let me fuck you in the ass."

Loud sobs: "But I didn't really want him to. Not really. And it really hurt, like my ass was ripping up . . . but even while my ass was hurting I felt delighted that I was hurting you by letting him hurt me so bad. Which sounds crazy, I guess."

Jane paused, breathing heavily. Kirk scratched his nose and waited for her to go on. He had a mental image of her with mascara smeared down her cheeks and snot dribbling from her nose and running down over her lips into her mouth.

After a while, she resumed speaking: "And afterwards . . . the very next day I broke it off with Kirk—not that there was really anything going on between us—and I've neither seen nor spoken to him since."

This last was news to Mike. Not that it made any real difference to the death of their relationship. He didn't want Kirk's sloppy seconds. Kirk was the kind of guy who boasted about his conquests.

"C-c-can you for-forgive me, Mike?" Jane wept. "I-I-I'm r-r-really s-s-sorry and th-th-thanks for hearing me out just now. I'm not proposing that we get back together again—'cos I really think that what I did to you was unforgiveable—but I just don't want you thinking I'm a slut. I know it sounds like I'm passing the blame for my actions, but I really did feel like I was under a spell at the time it happened. Right now, what I did with Kirk makes no sense to me. I don't even like him!"

She felt like she was under a spell. Once more feeling chilled, Mike looked over at the dining room, where he'd dropped Master Slim's business card on the table.

"Yes, I forgive you, Jane," he said. "What happened was unfortunate, that's all, 'cos I really liked you."

Her sigh of relief was audible. "You do? You really mean it?"

"Yes, I do. I totally forgive you. Weird stuff like that happens to people sometimes. I think that's why movie stars never stay married for long."

"We can still be friends, right? I'm not saying I wanna be your girlfriend or anything, but we're still friends, right?"

Mike nodded. "Yeah, that's cool." And then, before she could reply, he quickly added, "Hey, Jane, I need to hang up now. There's something I need to take care of."

"You're just trying to get rid of me, aren't you?" she said accusingly. "You haven't forgiven me at all."

"No, no, I'm not trying to get rid of you. Trust me—I really have to attend to his. Hey, we're friends again. You can call me whenever you like, or chat with me, or even visit me at home whenever you want. But I really, really, *really* do need to attend to something right now."

"Okay, thanks! I feel so much better now!" Jane said brightly and hung up.

She'd barely gotten off the line before Mike was up and hurrying towards the dining room to get Master Slim's card.

He didn't believe what he'd just heard. And he felt more spooked than ever before.

Thankfully Master Slim answered the phone almost immediately. After hearing Mike's reason for calling, he replied that sure, it was fine if Mike drove over right away.

Mike listened to the old man's directions to his place and then hurriedly got dressed and left home.

CHAPTER 5

Master Slim lived up in the northern part of Raynham, across the Blue Star Memorial Highway (aka I-495), and on the left if you were headed up to Brocton. This outskirts area of Raynham was mostly forest and farms, and Mike saw few other buildings along the dirt turnoff that led to the house.

The house itself was old, but in good repair. It looked like a farmhouse, though the area surrounding it was all uncultivated and seemed to have been that way for decades. Mike parked near the head of the driveway, beside a black Toyota sedan.

Mike apparently wasn't Master Slim's only visitor. As he got down from his pickup truck, the front door of the house opened and a young woman walked out.

She was a redhead, dressed entirely in black—black tee shirt, black skirt and leggings, black boots—and as she drew closer to him he saw that her makeup was all black too. She also wore a silver witch's star as a pendant.

"Hi," he greeted as she reached him. He assumed that the black Toyota sedan was hers.

"Hi," she replied with a half-frown. She was very attractive, but her green eyes flashed angrily at him; she was clearly pissed off about something.

He made no further attempts at conversation. She stepped past him, got into her car and drove off.

Mike stared after her for a few moments and then walked up to the house.

***

Master Slim was an aged man, tall and stooped and with deathly pale skin that both looked as flimsy as parchment and yet as tough as leather. He was bald with a fringe of white hair, had watery blue eyes, a large nose and thin lips, and his jaw was square. He'd been handsome once, that was certain, but time had since engraved its ugly lines on him.

The old man stood there at the front door in his white shirt and faded jeans, studying Mike for a few moments.

Then, "Come on in, son," he said in a faint sandpapery voice, turning away from the front door and gesturing before him into the house.

Mike followed him inside.

The house interior was clean and neat, with very little evidence of occultism except for two morbid paintings hanging on the walls, but Mike still felt ill at ease being here.

He felt silly now; his natural skepticism had reasserted itself during the drive over.

I'm in a magician's house—visiting a occultist—because I believe I might've been cursed? This is crazy! I'm crazy for listening to Bob and Jane, but . . .

Somewhere in the house, a radio or stereo was playing music at a low volume. It was a creepy sound—a chanting female singer backed by an organ and percussion. The singer sounded like she was worshipping the devil or some other deity that slumbered in dark realms that eschewed sunlight.

"Have a seat," Master Slim said. "No, not that chair, that one's my consulting chair. And besides, it's got a bad leg. You gotta know how to position yourself in it or you'll wind up on your ass. Sit yourself on the couch."

Mike seated himself on the couch instead.

A moment later, the old man seated himself on the chair with the bad leg, which stood next to the couch. The bad leg was the rear left one; it wobbled and Master Slim kept up a balancing act to sit on it comfortably. "I'se asked my son Dave to get this damn chair fixed more than once, but even though he's twice taken it off to a carpenter, each time he brings it back it seems in worse condition than before."

That said, the old man spent a short while closely studying Mike, with his age-lined face becoming as immobile as a marble carving.

His scrutiny made Mike very uncomfortable, which finally made him pull out his wallet.

"Sir, my friend said your consultation fee is a hundred dollars?"

The old man waved the comment aside. "Let's not talk about money yet; put your wallet back in your pocket." He frowned. "You got problems, son. Big problems indeed. I can sense them just by looking at you."

"What do you sense, sir—I mean, what do you see?"

Mike had figured this question was the acid test here. *If Master Slim can tell me exactly what is wrong with me, then I'll stay; if not I'll leave. I'll pay him his C-note and drive off. According to Bob, this old man is psychic . . . and Bob also said he didn't tell Master Slim's son Dave the true details of my predicament. So the only way he'll possibly know my specific tragedies is if he really is psychic.*

"Hold on a minute while I fish out the details," Master Slim said. After saying this, he was silent for a while. During that time he waved two fingers in a circle in front of Mike's face, closed his eyes and hummed softly to himself; a monotonous eerie chant.

In fact, the old man sounded as spooky as the music playing in the background, the eldritch melody of which now gave Mike chills. The singer sounded like she was being tormented by demons . . . and as if her wailing voice—this recording of her deepest agony—was opening a portal to the world of the dead.

Mike was relieved when Master Slim opened his eyes again.

"Well, first of all I'll tell you your symptoms," Master Slim said. "Your past three relationships have been . . . Lyn, the most recent girl lost her head in a car crash; Janie, the one before her was cornholed by a housemate of yours and ran off with him . . . and Ashley, the one before her, killed herself by ripping her guts out over a photo of you."

Master Slim smiled coldly at Mike. "How'm I doin' so far?"

"You're right," Mike admitted. "Bang on the money."

Master Slim nodded. "That's just to let you know I ain't a charlatan. You believe in me now?"

Mike nodded.

"Okay, now you can hand me that hundred dollar consultation fee."

Mike hastily got out his wallet and handed the money over.

Master Slim put the hundred dollars in a book on the table behind him and then turned back to Mike.

"Now brace yourself, son. What I'm about to tell you ain't pretty listenin', not pretty at all. That first girl, Ashley who killed herself?—I saw the news on the TV by the way—well, the reason she killed herself like that was to ensure you never had a happy relationship with a woman again."

Mike gasped.

Master Slim nodded. His facial expression now was grim; as black as the clothes of the young woman Mike had just encountered outside his house. "Yeah, that's the truth, son. I dunno where she found that ritual, but I hear everything's available on the internet nowadays . . . but she's got you good with it. The noose is as tight as a virgin's cooter around your neck."

For a few seconds Mike had no idea what to say or think. The spooky music had stopped playing in the background, which he was thankful for, but what he'd just heard was just too horrible.

"What can I do about it?" seemed to be the only logical question.

Master Slim shrugged. "Well, you've two options."

"Yeah?"

"First one—you can turn gay. Her spell only applies to relationships with women . . ." Then, seeing the disgusted look on Mike's face, he laughed. "Nah, son, I'm just jokin'; you don't strike me as swingin' that way."

"No I don't. What's the other option? And please don't tell me I've gotta remain celibate till I die."

Looking serious again, the wizened old man rubbed a hand over his bald and wrinkled head. "No, you don't have to do without a woman. I can fix your problem." While Mike sighed in relief, he went on: "You're lucky that she didn't know the whole spell; if she'd completed it, you'd be screwed for life. Turning gay would've been your only chance of having a love life."

Mike heaved another sigh of relief. "So, sir, what do we do now?"

The old man got to his feet and gestured to Mike to remain where he was. "Hang on a moment while I fetch a few things and slot in a fresh CD of music." He looked pointedly at Mike. "Yeah, and before we get started, this is gonna cost you two thousand dollars."

Mike laughed. "Sir, in this case, money is no object."

CHAPTER 6

Master Slim hummed along for a few seconds with the new evil-sounding CD he'd slotted into the hidden stereo, which to Mike sounded even creepier than the first one had. While absent the old man had also switched his plain white shirt for a black top with long sleeves and a red collar and red cuffs.

Mike waited and watched. There was no chance of him quitting now. He was filled with an intense expectation, though he couldn't have explained what he expected to happen. However, he was fully convinced that he was in the right place, and that this aged man held the solution to his problem.

Okay, so yes, that long black knife that Master Slim had brought out from the inner room did bother him a little.

"We're gonna need some blood from your arm," the old man explained.

The living room looked a bit different now. Master Slim had moved both his dodgy-legged consulting chair and the coffee table out of the way to make space for another, more ornate square table which he'd wheeled over on its castors from the corner near the bookshelf. Seeing the amount of effort the old man was putting himself to, Mike wondered why he hadn't simply dedicated a room in his house to his paranormal work.

Finally Master Slim was properly set up. On the square table he had arranged the black knife and a wooden cup carved in the shape of a human skull.

"Now we begin," the old man said, stepping up to the table on the opposite side from Mike. "What's Ashley's full name?"

"Ashley Cummins."

"You know her middle name? We need that too, so we don't summon the wrong ghost."

"Brooke," Mike replied. "Ashley Brooke Cummins."

Master Slim nodded, and then after humming along some more with the creepy singer, he indicated to Mike to get to his feet and then began the ritual.

***

Afterwards, Mike couldn't have said much about what had happened.

Master Slim had begun chanting a spell and the room had seemed to darken, like it was filling with fog, and the eerie music had gotten louder, with a rock guitar solo that seemed to go on forever, played on a scale that both ascended to heaven and descended to hell . . . and then, while both he and the aged occultist seemed to fade slightly, Ashley Cummins was suddenly there in the room with them.

It was unmistakably she.

Mike was understandably shocked and horrified by the amount of mutilation she'd inflicted on herself just to get even with him. Her belly gaped open and her intestines hung down over her pubis.

Despite her wounds, Ashley seemed neither angry nor sad. She glanced at Mike without emotion and then focused her attention entirely on Master Slim. They seemed to speak for a long while; though in actuality time now seemed as stretchable as a rubber band, and they might have conversed for less than a second. Mike didn't understand a word they said. Just like the music had gotten louder, their voices seemed to get quieter each time he tried to listen in on their conversation. But they were clearly negotiating a deal of some kind.

Finally, Ashley nodded. Then she pointed at the gaping hole in her belly and nodded towards Mike.

Then the old man seemed to walk through the table and Mike was aware of a sudden sharp pain in his right forearm and of the skull-shaped cup filling up with blood . . . and then the old man was once more on the other side of the table, handing the cup full of his blood to Ashley. Mike however felt faint; the living room seemed to whirl around him and he had to place a hand on the square table to keep from falling down.

Meanwhile, the singer's amplified chants and her demonic drum accompaniment throbbed painfully in his head.

Ashley sipped the blood and then she turned and smiled at Mike, her smile chilling him because her spectral teeth were now painted a dripping red. She finished drinking the blood and handed the cup back to Master Slim. As the room faded in and out around the three of them—the dead and the living—Ashley pointed to Mike and said something to Master Slim, who nodded back at her . . .

"Of course," he seemed to be agreeing.

And then, in a blink of Mike's eyes, Ashley Brooke Cummins was gone again.

The room whirled faster. Mike stepped back until his knees hit the couch and then he allowed himself to fall back onto it. Then he passed out.

***

Mike didn't know how long he was out for, but he awoke to find Master Slim once more sitting in his dodgy-legged consulting chair. He must have been unconscious for a while though, because the old occultist was once more wearing his white shirt and the square table was back in its place in the corner behind Mike.

The one constant was the eerie music, though it sounded like another fresh CD—this lady singer didn't sound as miserable as the previous one; her voice mingled pleasure and pain in varying amounts. Actually, she sounded like she was having sex with the devils.

The old man was shaking Mike's arm and his unstable chair wobbled precariously as he did so. "Wake up, son, it's done."

With that motivating news, Mike revived quickly.

"It's done? For real?" he asked, half breathless with relief.

The old man nodded, but he wasn't smiling, which put a damper on Mike's delight. "Sir, what's the matter? Like I said, the money isn't any object. Two thousand bucks, right? Just text me your bank account details and I'll wire you the money by tomorrow evening."

Master Slim laughed then. "Oh, it's not that, son. I trust you for the money, but there's something else—something that I hadn't foreseen." He shook a gnarled, liver-spotted hand at Mike's worried expression. "No, no, no, it ain't that—Ashley Cummins did agree to let you off the hook, but she wanted something in return from you."

"But she got something—she drank my blood," Mike protested. He remembered now how large that skull-cup had been and that it had been full to the brim with his blood and realized that the draining was the reason he'd passed out after the ritual was concluded. He peered down at his right arm now. Master Slim had stuck a Band-Aid over the wound, which was just above his wrist. Considering the amount of blood that he'd lost, this treatment seemed woefully inadequate to Mike, but it seemed to have worked—he wasn't bleeding anymore and could hardly feel the pain of the knife's gash.

He looked back at Master Slim. "Ah . . . alright, you can tell me the bad news, sir. Exactly what does Ashley want from me now?"

The old man burst into laughter then, which surprised Mike. "Hey, I thought this was serious," he protested.

"It is," Master Slim agreed, managing to restrain his laugher. "It's very serious, but not at all in the way that you imagine."

Mike had no idea what to expect, so he kept quiet. At least the old guy had said Ashley's demands weren't too serious.

"Well, it's like this, son," Master Slim said finally, his wizened face shining in his mirth and tears threatening to spill from his washed-out blue eyes. "Ashley Brooke Cummins says that she forgives you completely from the depths of her heart . . . and that you can have happy relationships again, but only . . . only . . ."—the old man seemed on the verge of bursting into laughter again—"but only—and she means this—only if from now on you *only* date girls who are named either Brooke or Ashley."

Mike stared at him. "What!? For-for-for r-r-real!?"

Master Slim nodded. "Yes, that's what she demanded." He shrugged. "It was the best deal I could negotiate—she said she'll let you off the hook on that condition alone, that henceforth you date only either Ashleys or Brookes, girls who share her own names. The girls don't have to have both of her names, but they must have at least one of them. She views it as you professing your love for her even after her death."

Mike remembered what Ashley's ghost had looked like—with the slashed open gut and intestines hanging down to her knees—and almost sympathized.

"And the alternative is?" he asked moodily, though he already knew the answer.

"More deaths, more misery," Master Slim replied flatly, his voice now completely devoid of humor. "Those were her conditions; her drinking your blood made it an unbreakable covenant between the two of you."

Mike nodded. "I've really no choice in this matter, have I?"

Master Slim nodded back at him, then said softly. "No choice at all, son. As far as *your* love life is concerned, it's strictly Brookes and Ashleys for you from now on."

In the background, the demonic singer wailed on in a language that made no sense to Mike.

CHAPTER 7

By the next afternoon, Mike had come to terms with his new romantic predicament.

Though after leaving Master Slim's house, he'd tried to mentally debunk what had happened there, he found himself unable to. What had happened in that old building hadn't been illusory, the old man really had called up Ashley Brooke Cummins's ghost. She really had appeared and . . . a twinge of pain had made him examine his arm— yes, she really had drunk his blood.

Bob had been disappointed that Mike hadn't asked him along.

"Man, I just didn't wanna wake you up. And after Jane called me, I was in a rush to go see the old guy."

"Wow, dude, you saw her ghost. A real ghost! Wow, that's so frigging cool."

Bob also didn't see the imposed name restrictions as too much of a problem. "Brookes and Ashleys? There's loads of girls with either of those names. Dude, you're really lucky her name wasn't Penelope Mallory Cummins. Then you might never have a girlfriend again."

Mike managed to laugh at that. "Bob, you're overlooking the fact that from now on, approximately ninety percent of young American women are off-limits to me.

Bob had shrugged. "So, what's the difficulty? You only need one of them, right? But, yeah, yeah, I dig you, dude. It's a bitch—you meet a pretty girl and no matter how much she likes you and vice versa, if her name ain't either Ashley or Brooke, you'll be endangering her life by dating her."

***

Now, as Mike crossed the east-side parking lot of the McDonald's restaurant on the New State Highway (i.e. Route 44), he pondered on that last detail.

Maybe I can just join an online dating club. That's an easy way to filter out girls by their names. I can even join several dating clubs. No danger there for the girls.

He found it odd that since yesterday's consultation with Master Slim, his misery over Linda's death and his mourning for her had drastically reduced. He was very conscious of this fact: both his grief concerning his late ex and his happy memories of her had receded to somewhere in the back of his mind. Half of the time he didn't think of Linda at all—which was of course a relief, but was also slightly creepy.

Did Ashley have something to do with that? Master Slim said she wants my dedication to her after her death.

"Hey there! Wait up!"

Mike, McDonald's purchases in hand, stopped and turned to face the speaker.

It was the young woman from yesterday—the redhead he'd met outside of Master Slim's place. She was dressed the same as yesterday—black clothes and shoes and black makeup also—but this time she was smiling at him. She had a very nice smile, though her teeth were slightly yellow.

"Hi," Mike said coolly.

She grinned at him. "You remember me, right?"

"You'd be very hard to forget."

She looked at him queerly. "Is that good or bad?"

He laughed. "Very good." Then he shifted the bag of fast food from his right hand to his left and extended his right hand for a handshake. "I'm Mike, nice to meet you again."

"Mortika." She shook his hand. Her hand was quite small, with a black pentagram tattooed on the inside of her wrist.

Now it was Mike's turn to stare queerly at her. "Mortika?"

She laughed, fingered her pentagram pendant, and pointed across the highway, at one of three shops in a building directly opposite them; a building situated a short distance from the Dam Lot Brook.

Mike read the black, star-splattered shop sign: 'Mortika: Jewelry, Fortunes and Spells.' He looked back at her. "Wow."

"It's really a Goth jewelry shop, but I do cast spells too." She laughed again. "So don't you dare piss me off, man, or I'll hex you real good." Then she added: "So, Mike, what brings you down this way, other than a late lunch?"

He shrugged. "I work at the Cashstretch Superstore down the road; I'm the most junior manager in the electronics department there."

She nodded. "And you just finished your shift and don't have any food at home, and you don't have a wife either, so . . ."

He nodded too. "You're really perceptive."

She grinned. "Nah, I'm just winging it—my psychic abilities are total shite. I'm nothing like Master Slim, but . . . you're not wearing a wedding ring and you don't seem particularly happy, so I figured 'no girlfriend' would be just right."

It finally occurred to Mike that this young Goth woman liked him; liked him in a 'potential girlfriend' way. He sighed. She was really attractive, with her green eyes seeming to hoover him into themselves. But of course he had to think of her safety.

And I'm just starting out with this. Just how many other lovely girls am I gonna have to avoid?

"Hey, you're looking sad again," Mortika said.

He tried to switch the topic: "You didn't seem particularly happy when I met you yesterday at the old man's house. What was that about?"

Her grin faded a little. "Oh, that was just a witch-to-witch consultation. But I didn't like what he told me."

Mike thought she'd just evaded answering the question, but he also realized it wasn't really any business of his. "Hey, look," he said. "It's been great meeting you again, but I've really gotta run. I need to—"

But Mortika's smile had already returned. "Hey, man, I've a great idea. Why don't you come have your lunch over in my shop? Business is really slow at the moment and we can get to know each other better."

Before Mike could protest, she had linked her arm in his and was leading him across the road.

***

Mortika's shop was wall-to-wall filled with gothic-styled jewelry and paranormal paraphernalia. It contained racks and racks of skull-/pentagram-/corpse-engraved rings and earrings, bangles and necklaces, hairpins and nose rings. There was a shelf of black cosmetics and a side alcove filled with what struck Mike as bondage gear. The glass display under the cash register held crystal balls, tarot cards and eerily realistic plastic skulls. And then there was the bookcase, which in addition to containing works by Aleister Crowley and Erin De Mornay also contained magic instruction DVDs.

She led Mike past all of these into a small office in the rear that had lots of gruesome paintings and movie posters hung on its walls.

"First off," she told him once he was seated, "Mortika is just my professional name, my real name is Ashley Richard." She giggled. "Ashley Jane Richard." Misinterpreting Mike's surprise at this revelation, she went on: "Yeah, don't I know it too? Ashley is a such total crap name for a witch . . . and Jane don't sound much better either. I mean, if my parents had named me Diana or Rhiannon or Elizabeth or Erin even, I'd not have minded, but no . . . hey, Mike, you're not eating your food."

He pushed the packages toward her. "I was thinking you might wanna share it with me."

This was untrue. What Mike was actually thinking about was how soon he'd managed to hook up with another 'Ashley.' Maybe Ashley Cummins was watching over him from the afterlife?

"Oh, I'm not really hungry," Mortika protested. "I'm watching my weight."

Mike made eye contact with her and said. "Your weight seems perfectly fine to me."

She smiled coyly back. Mission accomplished on both sides.

"I've always been interested in darkness," Mortika said after they'd split the burger in two. "Call me weird if you like, but I don't understand the human obsession with happiness. Most of us aren't really happy, and darkness lurks under our surfaces, almost like those images that we sometimes think we see out of the corner of our eyes."

"Like ghosts?"

She licked ketchup from her lips and shook her head. "Not really. Darkness is like the hidden portion of an iceberg, always there but unnoticed until we crash into it—something happens and we snap and lose our minds and blow our brains out or go on a killing spree. You read about that sort of inexplicable craziness all the time."

Mike nodded. He felt comfortable with her. He liked her red hair and her green eyes and her black-painted lips and her intensity. He'd never dated a Goth girl before. Goths had always struck him as snobs except when hanging out with other Goths, but Mortika—Ashley Richard—seemed down-to-earth enough.

The only problem I foresee is, what are we gonna have in common? What are we gonna talk about?

However, at the moment subjects of conversation didn't seem limited, as Mortika was quite loquacious. "I cringe nowadays when I see photos of myself as a teenager," she said. "There's one really wack one of me aged thirteen with my hair dyed black and my eyebrows shaved off . . . I mean you should see it. I then drew in these huge fake eyebrows with an eyebrow pencil—they were bigger than McDonald's' golden arches—ha ha ha! My poor mom had a fit the first time she saw them; my dad wanted to send me to a shrink. Hold on a minute and I'll find the photo for you in my cellphone . . ."

By they time they had finished sharing Mike's lunch, romance was unmistakably in the air, and he asked: "Hey, you wanna go see a movie tomorrow night?"

She nodded. "Oh, I'd love to, man. But where? And what are we gonna go see?"

"I don't know what sort of movies you like." Mike gestured out into the shop. "Somehow, I don't think chick flicks will appeal to you much."

That made her laugh out loud. "You're right, man . . . I don't really do those. Hey, how about going to see *Gore, Gore, Gore?* It's currently showing at the Abyss Club Theater in Taunton."

Gore, Gore, Gore?

"Yeah, that works for me," Mike quickly agreed.

***

"Dammit, dude, you're a fast worker," Bob said when Mike told him about Mortika. "That's less than twenty-four hours later. You're almost as fast as Kirk."

"No one is as fast as Kirk," Mike corrected. "I don't think even God could talk a woman out of her pants as fast as Kirk can." He shrugged. "I've just been lucky twice in a row that the girls I've chatted up liked me too. And Mortika practically hit on me, not the other way around." He grinned. "She's really cute though. Those eyes . . ."

"What are her tits like?" Bob leered. "What kinda rack she got?"

"I didn't notice. She had on this puffy witch-blouse—you know those old-style tops? It made her chest seem bulky."

"Dude, let's hope the bulk isn't just air and fabric."

They left it there. At the moment Bob didn't have a girlfriend. Anita, his last girlfriend, had left him for a fitness trainer who worked at 3M, the gym down the road from the Cashstretch superstore where Mike worked.

Bob however, was lackadaisical about hooking up again so soon afterwards their breakup. Not because his heart was broken, but as he put it: "Dude, it's the current job. Night-stocking plays havoc with night fucking. That was the main reason Anita gave for leaving me— either I was too tired to screw or she was."

Mike researched the movie *Gore Gore Gore* online. It was said to be 'completely nihilistic and over-the-top violent with witches and devils galore,' but the ratings were high in the Goth community.

Ah, it'll be worth it, to be with her, he thought, and spent the rest of the evening daydreaming about how great it would be to hold Mortika in his arms and kiss her.

***

At about 8 p.m. that evening however, Mike got a phone call from Master Slim.

"Hello, sir," Mike said brightly. "Thanks so much for yesterday. I've wired the money to—"

"Nah, son, that ain't why I called ya. There's something else I wanna tell you."

The old man's gravelly voice wasn't unfriendly, but it had a mark of unmistakable seriousness in it that immediately set Mike on edge. In addition, the unmistakably occult music playing in the background increased his disquiet. Mike began hoping that Ashley Cummins hadn't just reappeared from the grave with another stringent condition concerning his romantic happiness.

"I'm listening, sir," he said.

"Okay, son. It's about that girl you're plannin' on dating, the one you met outside my house yesterday."

"Mortika?"

"Yeah, yeah, her."

"What about her?"

"Yeah, I know she fits your current girlfriend criteria, but I'm tellin' you to break off that relationship. Break it off right now, before it even gets started. Do you hear me?"

Mike stared into the distance, seeming to see through the walls of his bedroom into the woods beyond. "But . . . why? She's an Ashley!"

"Yeah, I know she's an Ashley. Hey, listen, son—here's the thing: You gotta first understand that I can't tell you *why* you gotta break it off with her, 'cos that's private and personal, but I assure you that you don't want her."

"But I do; I really do want her! She's wonderful! She's—!"

"She's *wrong* for you. Break it off, Mike. I'm telling you this not as a businessman, but like I'd do for my own son Dave. Trust me, son, you'll thank me later."

Master Slim hung up before Mike could protest further. Mike lowered the phone and then sat staring at its screen for a while, while his mind furiously crunched over what he'd just heard.

Damn, ain't this a kick in the balls? he thought.

CHAPTER 8

Despite Master Slim's warning, Mike dilly-dallied all through Tuesday.

He really didn't want to break up with Mortika. Not that he was dating her yet, of course; this would be their first date, but . . .

But I like her. I like her so much. I really, really, do like this girl! He'd already begun daydreaming of introducing her to his parents up in Dover and of a nice Goth wedding and a nice Goth house with cute Goth kids and several black cats and . . .

But the occultist's warning echoed through his mind: *Break it off, Mike. I'm telling you this not as a businessman, but like I'd do for my own son Dave . . .*

The sincerity in that statement was hard to ignore. Even harder to ignore was the fact that the old man had somehow known that he'd asked Mortika out.

Yeah, I'd better do like he says, Mike finally decided. *I don't know why he's warning me off her, but I'd better listen to him.*

When Mike's work shift ended, he made a point of not driving past Mortika's shop, in case she noticed his pickup truck and wondered why he hadn't stopped to say hi. He took another route home.

He had however promptly and enthusiastically responded to the text messages she'd sent him at work. *Yes, I'll pick you up at seven. No, leave your car. There's no point taking both of them . . . etc . . .*

In theory, it should have been easy enough for Mike to simply claim that he was too busy to go out tonight, and rain-check their next meeting, but he didn't dare do that. And his reason was that now that he had agreed to break off things with Mortika, he suddenly felt very scared of her. No matter from which angle he considered what he had to do, he couldn't help visualizing a replay of what had transpired after he'd broken up with Ashley Cummins.

Yes, Mortika and I haven't yet even sat in the same car together, let alone kissed, but well . . . she's a witch, right?

Mike's problem was that if Ashley Cummins, who apparently had no knowledge of witchcraft other than an incomplete spell that she'd googled up, could fuck up his life so badly, what would an actual practicing witch, one who knew exactly what she was doing, be able to accomplish if *she* was mad at him?

Mike didn't want to take the chance of Mortika becoming so mad at him that she'd hex him too. *What'll happen then? I'll have an epileptic fit each time a woman smiles at me? Or my dick will fall off?*

He tried calling Master Slim to discuss his fears, but the old man's phone was switched off. Either the occultist was busy with a client, or the phone had run out of power, or he wasn't ready to discuss the matter any further with Mike, or . . . he'd fallen asleep or . . . or . . . whatever . . .

Anyway, Mike felt a sense of encroaching doom as the night and his date with Mortika grew closer.

***

"Hey, dude, why're you looking so glum?" Bob yawned when Mike got home from work.

Bob had a towel wrapped around his waist and was drinking a glass of milk. "You've broken off tonight's date with Mortika, right?"

Mike shook his head and told Bob what the problem was.

"Hey, that's a valid worry, dude. You know how they say hell had no fury like a woman scorned? Well, a witch scorned would be six-six-six times both more furious and more hellish. Dude, I don't wanna be you right now." He put the emptied glass down on the dining table and scratched his crotch through the towel. "Hey, better call Master Slim again. Maybe he'll answer the phone now."

Mike tried, but still couldn't get through. Aw, and this should be so simple, if he could just have Master Slim reassure him that his proposed action wouldn't have negative consequences.

This is crazy, he thought. *Here are both Bob and myself talking about me being hexed again as if . . . as if—*

"Hey, I've got it!" Bob suddenly exclaimed into Mike's dark thoughts.

"What?"

Bob grinned. "Dude, all you've gotta do is introduce Mortika to Kirk."

Mike frowned at his best friend. "What the hell do I wanna go and do something dumb like that for?"

Bob scratched in his mussed blonde hair and nodded enthusiastically back at him. "Listen, dude, this is a perfect solution. Pretty as you say this girl is, there's no way that Kirk won't try to steal her from you. He's gonna hit on her the moment you guys walk in through the door. And once that happens, it's an automatic breakup for you and you're not to blame for it. If she falls for Kirk, you're *completely* off the hook." He frowned. "But, here's the catch—dude, you gotta do it tonight, before you guys attend the movie. If anything romantic happens and you start kissing . . . well, from what I've heard, those witchy girls tend to be very, very faithful—apparently they stick like glue if they love you."

Mike doubted that a film titled *Gore, Gore, Gore* would have any romantic scenes, but he agreed that a Goth girl like Mortika might be turned on by the kind of over-the-top violence that the movie reviews promised.

So, yes, it's best that I do what Bob suggests.

He nodded to Bob and got out his cellphone. "I'd better call Kirk and let him know I'll be stopping by later."

Bob nodded. "Tell him you wanna borrow one of his porno DVDs."

Mike scowled at him. "Hey, gimme a break here. I'm not going to call Kirk and tell him I want to borrow his porno DVDs. The way he'd recount it to everyone, I'd never live it down."

"Ok, ok, so instead tell him you're dating this new freaky chick who loves horror movies and you wanna borrow his brother Eddie's *Halloween* movie box set."

"Does Eddie actually have a box set of *Halloween* DVDs?"

"Doesn't matter. It's simply a plausible reason for stopping by their place." Bob grinned. "And then you leave the rest to male and female hormones."

CHAPTER 9

When Mike picked up Mortika for their date that night, he almost quit on the plan. She looked utterly stunning. Hair, clothes, makeup, fingernails—she still looked 'dark' and 'gothy' but now she looked like a Goth queen.

Mortika had clearly gone to some extent to look her absolute best for him and it was hard not to appreciate the effort she'd put in; and to regret what had to be done tonight.

Aw shucks! Let's just get this over with, he thought grimly, while smiling as brightly as he could at her.

She was fine with stopping over at 'a friend's place first.' It was just seven-thirty. Lots of time to have dinner before *Gore, Gore, Gore* began.

Kirk and Eddie were both home, but they had a female guest with them. Blonde, slightly plump but very pretty, the young woman was sitting beside Kirk and she jerked her red skirt down over her knees as Eddie led Mike and his date into the living room. Kirk had his hand on her thigh and was whispering something into her ears but she looked upset, which wasn't the usual state of affairs with girls in Kirk's company; girls usually looked overjoyed that Kirk was pawing them. Kirk though, was just being himself; he didn't seem to notice the blonde's discomfort.

Kirk looked up and waved at Mike. "Hi, man, glad to see you're bouncing back again." And then his eyes focused on Mortika; they seemed to zoom in on her like binoculars. "Hey, who's the lovely lady with you?"

Mike felt really bad as he introduced Mortika to Kirk. But what had to be done, had to be done. Once they shook hands, he just sat back and watched things play out.

Yes, while with Mortika, Mike had constantly felt as if he was being vacuumed into her green eyes and sucked into her witchy aura, but now the case was reversed: he watched Mortika's eyes flare up as she was herself consumed by Kirk's animal magnetism.

Kirk instantly seemed to forget the girl seated beside him on the couch. From that point on Mortika had his full attention. The blonde girl noticed it too; and where before she'd merely been displeased over something or other Kirk might have done or said to her before Mike and Mortika's arrival, now she was visibly livid.

To salvage her dignity, she began talking to Kirk's brother Eddie, who was seated in the armchair beside her and was fiddling with the TV remote, trying to make up his mind between MTV and a wrestling show.

Eddie looked past her, saw what was happening between Kirk and Mortika and flashed her a sympathetic smile. Eddie was a nice kid. Though also sharing Kirk's dark good looks, he was nothing at all like his sleazy deadbeat brother. Eddie had a good job and actually contributed to the mortgage payments for the house and to putting food on the table, unlike Kirk who just sponged off their father. Eddie could have been a hit with the ladies too if he wasn't so shy.

Mike recalled that Eddie been very good friends with the late Ashley Cummins, so much so in fact that he'd wished the kid would chat her up and get her off of his back. Eddie had clearly liked Ashley back then, but unfortunately, as in lots of cases, the feeling hadn't been mutual—Ashley had only had eyes for Mike, with the current tragic series of consequences.

Kirk got up and invited Mortika into the kitchen. "Hey, babe, let's get some beers for everyone!"

They departed the living room and shut the door behind them. The blonde girl looked utterly furious at the desertion. Mike tried not to look relieved. Eddie was looking at the TV. He'd settled on a music channel, but was keeping the volume down, because the channel was playing a 'Chill Bill' rap video and Eddie was mostly into emo stuff.

Loud laughter came from behind the shut kitchen door.

The blonde girl looked scathingly at Mike. "Hey, do something! Kirk's in there with your date! Are you waiting till he rips her clothes off?"

Eddie looked away from the TV and added: "Man, she's right; that just might happen. Maybe you should get in there and break them up. Remember Jane."

"Oh, that isn't likely to happen," Mike said calmly. "We're on our way to watch a movie." He gestured at the kitchen door. "But dammit, I really, really wish I've got what that guy has!"

The blonde girl looked away from him in disgust. She clearly felt he was just a loser who'd lucked onto a hot date and didn't mind being cuckolded at the beginning if he still got the girl in the end.

Mike waited patiently. After a while Kirk and Mortika came out of the kitchen together. Mortika's black lipstick was slightly smeared and Kirk's lips looked darker than normal, so they'd obviously been kissing in there. The pair handed beers around. The blonde placed hers on an end table and made a point of ignoring Kirk, who wasn't looking at her anyway.

Mike now felt really embarrassed for the girl. Weird thing here was that he could see that she—Kirk hadn't introduced her, so he didn't know her name—she was just as hot as Mortika was. Yes, so she was a little fleshy, but she wore it very well like some women did. She was definitely pretty though. And . . . Kirk must have thought she was good-looking too, or else he'd never have asked her out.

So why had Kirk lost interest in her so quickly then?

Oh, I get it—Kirk is primarily interested in Mortika because she's with me! Mike realized. *That's what's going on here. Kirk is interested in proving to me— well to himself really—that he's the alpha male here and that he can dominate me by taking my women at any time he chooses! So even though he already has one pretty girl, he's publicly ditching her to seduce MY pretty girl. Well, that's okay; it ain't like we're still friends except in his mind.*

"Hey, Mike?"

Mike nodded at Mortika, who was now seated on the arm of the couch beside Kirk. "Yes? Are you ready to leave?"

She grimaced and looked upset. "No, I'm sorry, man, but I don't feel up to making the movie anymore. I've got this raging migraine— my head's beating like Slain Jane are rehearsing inside it."

Mike nodded understandingly. "Hey, some other time then. How 'bout I run you home instead?"

Mortika shook her head and then grimaced, as if his offer of a ride home had increased the pain of her fictional headache. "Oh no, you don't need to bother about that; Kirk has offered to drive me home, but I wanna rest here a bit first."

Kirk's victorious smirk said it all: *Man, don't blame me. Can I help it if all the hot bitches want me and not you?*

Mike got to his feet. "Yeah, sure, I guess I'll run along then. Hey, give me a call when you're feeling better, huh? We can have lunch."

The blonde girl was staring at the TV with Eddie. She looked absolutely miserable. She clearly didn't want to accept defeat and leave. Mike took pity on her. If he didn't, Kirk might talk her into having a threesome with himself and Mortika. And the blonde would very likely go along with the suggestion, if only to prove to herself her desirability when compared to her redheaded opponent in the ongoing seduction battle. She'd hate herself in the morning, but would suck dick like a whore tonight.

"Hey," he called out to her. "Do you wanna go watch a movie with me?"

She didn't seem to hear him, or maybe she didn't want to hear him. But then Kirk nudged her viciously with his elbow. "Hey, Ashley, the guy's talkin' to you."

A feather could have knocked Mike down. *Her name is Ashley? Two of them in the same room?*

The blonde girl whirled around with enraged eyes. "Ouch, Kirk, that hurt! What? What is it? What do you want from me now?"

Kirk pointed to Mike. "Ashley, my friend Mike is asking you out."

Ashley looked at Mike, who politely explained, "Mortika doesn't feel up to going to the cinema anymore, so I'm wondering if you'd like to be my date instead."

Ashley sized Mike up and down. She was clearly wondering whether she could trust him or if he was simply another creep looking for an easy lay. But then Mike winked at her and she realized what he was really doing, helping her cut her losses and get out of here with some dignity.

So she replied, "Yeah, whatever. At least I'll be somewhere where I'm wanted, with a real gentleman, not some scumbag."

"Scumbag?" Kirk laughed. "Oh, you're breaking my dick, baby."

"You can't break something that's permanently limp," Ashley retorted.

Kirk laughed. "Oh, I'm so hurt by your sour grapes. Don't you wish you'd just made my dick go limp?"

Ashley got up and picked up her purse. "Fuck you, asshole. I hope this redhead bitch gives you an STD."

Now it was Mortika's turn to laugh, though she quickly faked misery again.

Ashley and Mike left the building.

CHAPTER 10

Outside the house, the sky was just beginning to gray now. There was maybe a half-hour of daylight left. The air was warm with the faintest suggestion of a breeze.

Once Mike closed the front door behind them, Ashley's frigid expression thawed and she regarded him with a grateful smile on her face.

"Thanks for getting me out of there," she said as they stepped down off the front porch. "I can't believe Kirk would publicly humiliate me like that after all his efforts to get me to come here."

Mike laughed. "That's Kirk the jerk for you."

"We weren't properly introduced in there. I'm Ashley Hunt. But, man, I'm really not in the mood to go watch a film right now."

"Mike Broadman. Oh, I'm sure you'd have hated the flick anyhow. How about having dinner with me then, to salvage both of our evenings?"

She shook her head. "Sorry, but I don't even know you . . ."

Mike laughed. "Yeah, I know. And I might be a rapist or serial killer or whoever."

She was silent. He'd guessed right.

Mike grinned. Her rejection didn't matter. He was too delighted at having unknotted the knotty Mortika issue to care. There was no chance of him being re-hexed now. "Ah, no problem. Hey, so long as you don't mind riding in my old pickup truck—it isn't flashy like Kirk's ride—I'll drive you home."

"Don't trouble yourself, I'll just call a Uber. That's how I arrived here."

"It's no trouble at all. Which part of town do you live?"

"Lakeview Drive."

"That's the way I'm going. Home to a solitary microwaved dinner . . . seeing as I'm denied the pleasure of your company."

"Okay, you can drive me home."

They were down by Mike's pickup truck now. Ashley looked curiously at him, then pointed back at the house. "Hey, you don't seem bothered that Morticia Addams . . . or whatever her name is . . . you don't seem bothered that she just dumped you for Kirk."

He nodded. "Yeah, I'm not really."

"She's a slut then?"

Mike grinned at her. "Well, if she isn't already, she's about to be."

The blonde grinned too. "*Men.* Hey, you aren't pimping for Kirk, are you?"

Mike shook his head vigorously. "Not at all. I don't even like Kirk anymore."

"So . . . ?"

"Look, you're reading way too much into this thing with Mortika. It's our first date. I'm just delighted that things went bad before they could turn toxic."

He opened up the driver's side door of the truck, got in and then leaned over and opened up the passenger door for her. "Get in and let's get out of here."

She climbed in and they drove off.

As he backed the truck into the street, he said, "You know I can't help thinking you look familiar in some way. Do I know you from somewhere?"

She smirked at him. "Really? That's a grossly overused pick-up line. Try something more original."

"No no no, I'm not trying to pick you up."

She laughed coldly. "Oh, you can. It's O.K. I'll go out with you . . . just not tonight. Or you'll have a totally depressed bitch on your hands."

Mike couldn't believe his luck. "Yeah, that's great. I'll call you on the weekend then. We can have dinner together."

"Yes, certainly. The weekend will be fine. I should be fully recovered from my Kirk-influenced man-hating phase by then."

"But hey, listen," Mike said, as he turned the corner off Kirk's street. Ashley lived just a few minutes away, across the Forge River. "I meant what I said: It really does seem like I know you from somewhere."

She looked sideways at him, her plump face pretty in the dusk, even though her lips were clenched tight in displeasure. "Oh? Really?"

"Yeah, for real. The image is a vague one though; like we've met, but we've not really met. Almost like a dream."

Her expression turned apprehensive. "You're scaring me now. That sounds weird and creepy. You sound slightly nuts. Maybe I should have taken that Uber after all."

Mike took his right hand off the steering wheel and snapped his fingers. "Ah, I get it now. You're a friend of Bob's, aren't you?"

She looked surprised. "Bob Evans? Lanky blonde guy who looks like a stoner?"

"Yeah, that's him. So . . . you know him?"

She laughed. "Sure, everyone in Raynham knows Bob. I work with him at Walmart. I'm a manager there."

Mike laughed too. This just got better and better. "It really is a small world. Bob Evans is my housemate. We've been friends since childhood. So you see, you really have nothing to fear from me."

"Hey, don't rub it in—a young woman cannot be too careful nowadays. I already agreed to go out on a date with you this weekend."

Grinning, Mike pulled into the driveway of her apartment building and parked the pickup truck. He turned to face her, his hands raised and his fingers wiggling in a mock scary gesture. "And now, pretty woman, it is the moment we've both been waiting for."

She backed away against the passenger door. "Hey, man, don't you dare try to kiss me. If you do I will scream so loud your balls will fall off."

"Ashley, I meant that it's time to exchange phone numbers."

She looked embarrassed—"Oh"—and then reached into her purse for her cell phone.

"Hey, are you always like this?" she asked worriedly.

"Like what?"

"I don't know. So hyper, I guess. It's like you're extremely happy. Hey, you're not on drugs, are you? Because I'm not into that at all."

Mike laughed. "Nah, I haven't smoked pot since high school. I'm high on you, girl. You have no idea how happy I am meeting you tonight. One doesn't run into women as pretty as you everyday."

Though she tried to hide it, he could see that she was blushing and that she was delighted by the compliment.

He actually thought that he could have leaned over then and kissed her and that she would have accepted his lips on hers without any protest. But then, again maybe he was wrong and she would have shrieked his balls off.

It was best not to push his luck. It was best to wait until the weekend.

She got out of the truck, shut the door, and leaned in through the window.

"Please do call me," she said with a bright smile. "I promise not to stand you up like your last date just did. You seem like a really nice guy and I do want to get to know you better."

"Sure thing, Ash, I'll definitely call you." He was struck by a thought. "Hey, Saturday is Bob's birthday; we're having a barbecue, a get-together with some friends. You could come over to the house and party with us."

She nodded. "Yeah, maybe. That sounds nice."

"Cool, then."

"I can't stand creeps like Kirk, guys who think that because they have a dick they own the world. But you, you're not like that at all. You seem to actually care about a girl's feelings."

Personally, Mike thought vaginas ran the world; men were totally at the mercy of pussy. Guys would do just about anything to get laid, even down to committing actual murder.

He grinned as he watched Ashley Hunt walk to the front entrance of the apartment building. She was nicely shaped, not exactly plus-sized, but very plush bodied. He could just imagine the satisfying feeling of squeezing up close to her curves.

"Kirk certainly lost out with this one," he thought aloud and with a warm sense of satisfaction as he swung the pickup truck out of Ashley's driveway and headed for home. "Wait till Bob hears about this in the morning."

***

As Mike pulled up into his driveway, his phone rang. It was Master Slim, with the now-familiar occult music playing in the background.

"Sorry I haven't gotten back to you earlier than this," the old man said in his raspy voice. "So, you done it yet?"

"Yeah, I just got home from doing it."

"Good, son, good. Trust me, Mike, you ain't gonna regret listenin' to me 'bout this."

The old man hung up. Mike grinned at the cellphone screen. *You don't know the half of it, old man. I've finally met the one girl in the world who's immune to Kirk's charms, and she's an Ashley too. How lucky can one guy be?*

CHAPTER 11

The next morning, Mike was having coffee when Bob got in from work.

Because Mike didn't want to seem too eager, he'd decided to put off calling Ashley Hunt even to say hello. Today was Wednesday, waiting till Friday couldn't hurt his prospects with her.

Delaying his getting in touch would also give her sufficient time to forget how angry Kirk had made her. He hoped it would also make her eager to see him.

He gave Bob the long version of what had transpired the previous night.

"Oh, Ashley's a great girl," Bob replied enthusiastically. Nice rack too. I wonder what she ever saw in Kirk."

"Same thing as all the rest of them see in him, I guess. Nothing."

" 'Nothing' must be really attractive to young women nowadays. Kirk's *nothing* has so far stolen two chicks from you, dude."

"Yeah, and today I'm so delighted about that."

Bob went off to sleep and Mike went off to work.

The day passed quickly and smoothly for Mike. He felt buoyed by his safe and seamless transition from one Ashley to another, was almost dancing as he attended to the customers in the Cashstretch electronics department. Even the few belligerent complainers couldn't dampen his mood.

Even so, he resolved not to drive past Mortika's shop for at least a week, just in case she spotted his car and suddenly (and miraculously) became filled with a desire to get back together with him again.

Yes, life was really looking up at the moment.

CHAPTER 12

Two days later—Thursday night—Ashley Hunt still felt very depressed over Kirk's treatment of her.

Oh my God, that was such a total disaster. I can't believe Kirk would ever treat me like a cheap hooker like that.

She'd just gotten in from work. Walmart today had been murder; everything had seemed to go wrong all at once and to crown matters off, halfway through her shift she'd noticed Kirk in the store, chatting up some other girl.

Seeing Kirk had totally ruined her day. Now she felt emotionally abused and exhausted.

Glass of wine in hand, she sat in her living room and tried to find something on the TV that would calm her. But it was no good; each chick flick she switched to merely reminded her of how badly Kirk had treated her.

Look, I'll go crazy if I remain in here with just the television and my thoughts! Oh heck, why hasn't Mike called me yet? I hope I haven't scared him off. Maybe I should have taken him up on his offer of dinner that night. He really seemed nice enough to date. He rescued me—he was like a frigging knight in shining armor. Oh, at least I could have invited him up for a drink. Then he'd have realized that I actually liked him and wasn't just trying to cool him off. If I'd done that, maybe I wouldn't be alone like this now, an emotional vulture picking at the bones of my romantic corpse.

But on that miserable Tuesday night, it had been necessary for her to salvage some pride.

Kirk, Kirk! Ashley wished she'd never set eyes on him. But . . . well . . she'd been at work and Kirk had been buying a pair of sneakers and . . . he'd been so damn handsome and she just had to know him better and . . . and . . .

And he dropped me like a rotten apple immediately that Goth bitch walked in!

It hurt. It hurt so damn much. She felt caged in between bars of rage and misery.

She got up from the armchair, picked up her purse and left the apartment again. As she got into the elevator, she made up a miscellaneous mental list of unneeded things to buy from the store at the corner. A completely superfluous list of course, since she worked at Walmart; but she needed an excuse to get out of the house for a while.

If she remained in her apartment any longer, she'd go insane with regret and misery.

A walk was certain to clear her head.

***

"Are you *still* mad about that? Listen, you really need to put it behind you. You already told me that you met another guy there . . . a nice guy this time."

Ashley laughed. "Yeah, I guess you're right. But, oh my God, Terri, I've never been so embarrassed in my damn life!"

"Wow, I still can't believe he really did that to you! What a douche."

"But . . . the other guy I met, he hasn't called me yet!"

A plastic bag of cleaning materials in her left hand, Ashley was heading back home now while chatting with her best friend Terri.

Ashley felt much better now. The walk and the fresh air had indeed helped spruce up her mood. The street was empty except for the random passing car, but the streetlights were on and she was less than a hundred yards away from her apartment building.

Sharing her resurgent disgust with Kirk with her friend was a huge help. Terri wasn't the kind of friend who'd gossip her awkward secrets to others.

"Oh, girl, I wished the floor would open up and eat me!" she told Terri.

"I can imagine the feeling. I've met some real creeps in my time too, but no one's ever done that to me before; switch me for another girl right while I was sitting there. I'd just die if they did!"

Swinging her bag, Ashley chatted on. She was almost home and she didn't imagine she'd have any trouble relaxing now. A problem shared really was a problem halved.

"Well, things did end well—thank heavens," she said and then sighed: "But, Terri, Mike hasn't called me yet. I'm starting to worry that maybe he won't."

"Don't give up hope yet, he may just be busy."

"I'm thinking that maybe I shouldn't have cooled him off when he asked me out that night. But I didn't want to appear too eager to go out with him like I'd done with Kirk."

"No, no, girl, you did the right thing. You don't want him to start treating you like dirt too. You can't let a guy think you're an easy lay . . . Hey, but all hope's not lost yet."

"Not lost? What do you mean?"

"Remember you told me that Saturday is Bob's birthday?"

"Yeah, I did. So . . . ?"

Terri giggled. "So, if Mike doesn't call, you can take the initiative . . . you can easily gatecrash Bob's birthday party at their house on Saturday, if you really want to see him. Just remember to buy Bob a birthday present so you don't give your real reason for being there away."

"Damn, Terri, you're so sneaky."

"Yes, I am, aren't I? But that's what I'd . . ."

Ashley Hunt suddenly felt a prickling sense of danger; one that seemed to race from zero percent worry to one hundred percent anxiety in six seconds.

She stopped and turned around. Something was wrong nearby, but what?

Then she understood what the problem was. A car was heading right for her, screeching up off the blacktop onto the sidewalk as she watched. The vehicle's headlights were off and, engrossed on the phone, she'd not heard its engine at all and so had had no idea that it was even behind her.

"NOOOO!" Ashley screamed as the black vehicle hit her head-on and her cellphone and bag of purchases flew from her hands and the car dragged her mangled body a short distance down the sidewalk and then crunched her beneath its tires as it slewed back onto the road and sped off out of sight.

After that there was shocked silence in the street, silence that was punctuated by her friend Terri's concerned voice on the phone: "Hey, Ash, what was that loud noise? Ash, Ash, say something—talk to me!

Are you okay? . . . Oh, my God, what's happened? Was that a car? Oh my God! Hey, Ash . . . Ash . . . ?"

CHAPTER 13

Mike was very surprised to receive a phone call from Bob on Friday afternoon. Knowing that Mike spent most of his day on his feet attending to customers, Bob hardly every called him at work. That fact alone made him realize that something serious was up when his phone kept buzzing in his pocket.

He ducked out into the corridor that ran behind the electronics department to answer the call.

"Dude, you're never going to believe what I just heard," Bob gushed over the phone in an agitated rush.

Even before Bob went on, Mike had a intense feeling of disorientation, as if the ground had suddenly been yanked out from under his feet.

No no no no no frigging no! he thought, though he had no idea what he was scared of hearing.

But his fear proved very justified.

"Dude, Ashley Hunt is dead."

"Dead? Bob, make sense! How can she be dead?" He realized he'd raised his voice and might end up drawing attention to himself even out here. He looked up and down the corridor, but no one was approaching.

"Hold on, man," he told his cellphone. Then he backed into a nearby storeroom, shut the door behind him and returned the phone to his ear. "Bob, what the hell do you mean that Ashley is dead?" he whispered.

Then he listened to Bob's reply, with his face slowly turning white from shock.

"Dude, Ashley was run over by a car last night. The cops say it was a hit-and-run accident. They're still looking for the killer car and its runaway driver."

"But . . ." Mike felt chilled and completely lost for words; he was wiping away tears from his eyes. "Bob, how . . . how . . . ? I was gonna call her this evening after work and invite her over for your birthday tomorrow."

Bob sounded depressed too. "Dude, I know. But according to the police, after she got home from work she left her apartment again . . . walked down the street to buy some stuff from the store at the corner . . . She was run down on her way home from the store. According to the cops, she was smeared all over the sidewalk. . . . Sorry, dude, I already knew how bad this was gonna shake you, but I just had to talk to someone after I heard the news."

Mike was silent, devastated by the news.

"Dude, you still there?"

"Yeah, I'm here—just speechless, is all. I'll see you later."

***

Mike spent the rest of the shift on autopilot. Over the course of the remaining two hours he took four bathroom breaks, each time solely to see if he could get Master Slim on the phone.

But just like on Tuesday, the old man was once again incommunicado. Mike wondered if this was a daily habit of Master Slim's, if he regularly switched his cellphone off in the afternoon so he could take a nap, which was understandable enough for a man of his age.

But if such was the case, right now the old man needed someone to shake him awake already.

I met Ashley Hunt barely two days ago, fixed a date with her and she's dead already? What on earth is happening?

Mike felt intensely frustrated. He was worried, and this was a worry that threatened to soon degenerate into full-blown terror if he did not quickly get an explanation of what was going on.

We performed the ritual, he thought desperately as he sat on the toilet seat with his pants still firmly pulled up and his belt buckled. *We performed that bloody ritual, so why the hell is Ashley Hunt dead now?*

It took a heroic amount of willpower to accomplish, but Mike managed to convey the false impression that he was still concentrating on work.

Once he got off shift however, he immediately drove his pickup truck up to the northern part of Raynham, heading for the old occultist's house.

CHAPTER 14

There were two vehicles parked outside Master Slim's house, a blue Ford pickup truck exactly like Mike's and a white Honda sedan.

At least the old guy seems to be home, Mike thought with relief as he alighted from the vehicle.

But even before he had stepped up onto the front porch he could tell that something was very wrong here. The first red flag was the blood spilt on the porch steps with footprints in it. The other thing was the wide open front door and the blaring infernal music, as if the old man had cranked his stereo system up to the maximum to terrify his neighbors. This CD sounded like the soundtrack to a horror film, tribal drumming mingled with male and female moans and screams.

Oh no! Mike thought in horror, pulling out his cellphone and dialing 911 while he carefully navigated his way around the blood on the floor. The smell of death welcomed him at the front door, and he could hear the flies buzzing around inside the living room.

"911. What is your emergency?"

Mike told the lady exactly what he was currently looking at and asked her to send the cops as fast as she could.

Inside the house was as bad as he had anticipated from the blood outside. There were body parts strewn everywhere; strings of guts on the couch; bloody lungs on the seat of the old man's rickety consulting chair; severed arms and legs stacked on the coffee table; a human liver placed on the square table in the corner near the bookcase . . . Everywhere he looked was a tapestry of gore.

There were several shattered beer bottles and drinking glasses strewn on the living room floor amidst the bloody mess of body parts, along with two half-full whiskey bottles.

Mike mistakenly stepped on a length of intestine. He winced as it squashed beneath his feet. The overloud mystic music sounded unnerving, but he felt rooted to the spot, too scared and confused to step into the adjoining room where the stereo was blaring from and turn it off.

He prayed that the cops would arrive soon.

While staring at this terrifying physical wreckage, Mike quickly realized two things:

One of these was that there were many more body parts in evidence than made up a single human being. At a glance from his safe vantage point on a bloodless portion of the living room floor, he easily made out five severed legs. Which meant that there were at least three dead people here, one of whom was certain to be Master Slim.

The second glaring thing here in the living room was the lack of human heads. There were none in evidence.

Mike looked to his left, into the room from which the music was coming. Then, like a fish being reeled in and unable to save itself, he stepped that way, the riddle of the missing human heads more intriguing than his fear.

There was more blood splattered in the inner room. The three missing heads were in there also, arranged in the middle of a pentagram drawn in blood in the middle of the floor.

Master Slim's decapitated head was instantly recognizable by its baldness. Mike hazarded a guess that a second, balding head belonged to Master Slim's son Dave. The third dead guy was likely just a friend of theirs.

Mike remembered the shattered glasses and bottles out in the living room. Somebody must have come in here while they were drinking and murdered them all.

The singer wailed miserably from the cranked up stereo. Her voice was so terrified that Mike had a clear impression of a woman being torn apart by devils, her limbs pulled off of their joints and cast out into the void; her body left to roast in hellish flames.

"Yeah, lady, we're both going through some real hard times," Mike said in sympathy with the suffering woman and then he walked outside to wait for the police.

CHAPTER 15

The police arrived speedily. However, one thing Mike hadn't considered before calling them was the nature of the questions they would ask him.

Of course he had expected to be questioned on how he'd found the bodies, but he had been too traumatized by the massacre to think clearly as to the detail of what those questions might be.

But in hindsight, he realized this was a good thing. Because, if he'd given it any real thought, he'd have simply driven away from Master Slim's place as fast as he could after finding the bodies, which would have automatically added him to the list of suspects.

Mike had previously met Detective Shania Banks when she'd walked into Cashstretch to inform him of Ashley Cummins's death.

She was a short woman with short red hair, and who seemed to be in her mid-thirties. Her lips were small and thin, her eyes large and green. However, unlike Mortika's eyes which had seemed like invitations to a pleasure palace (with the expected inflating results south of the waistline), Shania Banks' eyes made Mike think of mold-covered prison cells (also with the expected deflating results south of the waistline—looking at her, Mike could already imagine well-hung men raping his ass). In addition, both her face and her suit were creased by overwork. She looked like she'd been sleeping too little and drinking too much coffee.

"Not more goddamned deaths," she griped to Mike, after having pulled him away to sit in her brown Subaru SUV. She sat in the driver's seat, he next to her in the front passenger seat. She tapped the steering wheel with her left hand and then scratched her upper lip with it, revealing her wedding band. "I've hardly been home in weeks. At this rate my two kids are gonna forget what I look like and my husband's gonna get himself a mistress. Each time I step into our front yard I half expect our dog to mistake me for a burglar and bite me."

Mike nodded. He still hadn't recovered from what he'd seen in the house.

"So, what brings you here today, Mr. Broadman?" Shania Banks asked.

"What?" Mike asked. "I-I-I . . ."

"No, we don't suspect you of butchering those guys. According to Doc, they've been dead for at least eighteen hours."

"Eighteen hours? That's last night. Last night around midnight."

Shania Banks nodded. "Well, yeah. That fits in with our theory that they were drinking, were all maybe quite drunk, which was how the killers could so easily subdue all three of them. I'm sure you saw all the beer bottles on the floor."

"Yeah."

"And the bloodstains are all dried up too."

"I didn't notice that the blood was dry. I just noticed that there was a lot of it splattered everywhere. That was frightening enough for me."

Mike thought for a moment. "Hey, if they were killed last night, why's the stereo still playing?" Then he frowned. "No, don't bother answering that one—selling electronics is my job. I'd have figured the answer to that out quicker if I wasn't so flustered. They looped the damn CD, right?"

Shania Banks nodded and smiled. It was a very cold smile. "Now, Mr. Broadman, back to my initial question. Yeah, you've already told us that you came here to talk to Master Slim about something. But what exactly did you come here to see him for?"

Mike really didn't want to reply the question. "It's embarrassing to say."

Shania Banks clearly realized this, because she said, "Listen, okay? I don't see what's so unmentionable—people consult psychics all the time."

"Have *you* ever consulted a psychic, detective?"

She nodded. "Yeah, once. Our dog went missing and I was so worried I consulted a medium to locate him." She laughed. "The lady told me he'd just run off to get laid and he'd be back in about a week. And that was exactly what happened. So what's *your* story?"

"Off the record?"

She nodded. "Yeah, so long as you weren't asking him where you could safely bury a corpse so we won't find it."

So Mike told her what had been happening to him ever since Ashley Cummins's suicide, right up to Ashley Hunt being run down by a car last night.

When he was done speaking Shania Banks gestured through her windshield at the beehive of police activity that now surrounded Master Slim's residence and shook her head. "I'm sorry to ruin your theory of a magical spell harassing you, Mr. Broadman, but most of what you've just described can easily be written off as coincidence."

Mike nodded. Not wishing her to think him a crank, he had left out mention of the bloodletting ritual Master Slim had performed to summon Ashley Cummins, as well as the ghost's own appearance. He figured Detective Banks would see a clear difference between her enquiring about her missing dog and his calling up a ghost.

"Coincidence? Yeah, maybe," he agreed.

"Don't worry, we'll catch the scumbag who ran Ashley Hunt down. That's just a matter of time."

Mike also gestured out through the windshield of her SUV. "So . . . what . . . no, who . . . *is* responsible for Master Slim's death then?"

She shrugged. "Most likely drug dealers."

"Drugs?" Mike shook his head. "Ma'am, their heads are arranged inside a pentagram drawn on the floor in blood."

Shania Banks nodded and her green eyes seemed to grow even colder, as if they were trees shedding their leaves in preparation for winter. "Yes. It's a common diversionary tactic in the criminal world. Whoever killed him knew he was an occultist, so they made it look like he was killed by a rival occultist. Those guys all like making drug-related killings as bloody as possible to scare the competition."

Mike wasn't buying it: "Aw c'mon! Drugs? The old man seemed fully legit to me . . . even if the sounds he played were really scary."

Shania Banks waved a dismissive hand. "I don't mean Master Slim—the old guy probably had no idea what was going on. I'm talking about his son Dave. We've had Dave Brooks on our law-enforcement radar for a while now, as a connection for Marko Velli's dealers up in Boston."

Dave BROOKS? Mike hid his surprise well, and instead asked: "Marco who?"

A cold laugh: "Be glad you don't know who that is—such ignorance is certain to lengthen your life expectancy a good deal."

"Okay, and the third dead guy was . . . ?"

"Dave's Ohio connection. He's been ID'd as Louie Vellasi; works for a guy named Vince Collins—Marko's Ohio counterpart." She frowned. "It's my educated guess that we'll find a stash of drugs cached somewhere in the house—if the killers didn't locate them last night."

A tall uniformed cop was approaching the SUV. He looked pale.

Shania Banks nodded to Mike. "Probably coming to tell me they've located Dave's coke stash. "Okay, Mr. Broadman, that'll be all for now. We'll give you a call to come to the station if we need any further details from you.

"Yeah, sure." Mike nodded and got out of the brown Subaru SUV.

Shania Banks got out too. Mike heard the other police officer say, "We've found some cocaine, ma'am. The coke packets were concealed in the leg of one of the chairs in the old man's living room. The chair has a bad leg so you can't sit on it . . . killers would have had no idea . . . fell over while forensics were scraping the gore off of it and the coke spilled out."

As Mike walked off, he recalled Master Slim saying that he'd twice asked Dave to get his consulting chair fixed, but even though Dave claimed he had, the chair was even worse now.

Wow, his son was hiding coke in his consulting chair all this while?

Mike was relieved to be off the hook. But he felt very saddened by Master Slim's death. Not just because it meant the severing of a personal lifeline, but also because the old man had seemed like a genuinely nice person.

Shaking his head, Mike climbed up into his pickup truck and hit the road again.

As Mike departed the farm, his thoughts were perplexed ones. Despite Detective Banks' suggestion that Master Slim and his son's deaths were merely coincidental to Mike's current dilemma, he couldn't shake the worry that their surname—Brooks—held some relation to their deaths.

CHAPTER 16

Saturday evening. The weather was behaving itself, complying with what the seers who predicted it on TV had prophesied, and Mike and Bob's backyard was full of people.

Along with the smell of roasting meat, the sound of revelry filled the air.

Carefully, so that no one would notice their motion, Mike parted the drapes of his bedroom window a little and peeked out.

With the kind of sociable individual Bob Evans was, Mike wasn't at all surprised by the huge turnout for his twenty-eighth birthday party—neighbors, friends Bob had met both in the flesh and via the internet, Walmart work colleagues, several cousins from nearby towns and an ex-girlfriend or three. Mike figured that there were at least two hundred people out there in the backyard, laughing and dancing to the music that a DJ friend of Bob's was feeding them from a large sound system.

Today was gonna play hell on Bob's credit cards.

Mike caught sight of his recent ex Jane and of both Kirk and Eddie. Jane was standing under the large maple tree on the left of the backyard. She was holding a glass of red wine and was looking rather lost, though Mike didn't think she could be drunk this early in the evening. Eddie was being his usual quiet self, lounging anonymously around the edge of the festivities with a soft drink in one hand and a plate of grilled chicken in the other, while Kirk already had a leggy brunette leaning on his shoulders and hanging on every word he was saying.

So far Mike hadn't seen any sign of Mortika. It looked like she wasn't here. He assumed that, realizing her attending this party would certainly lead to several awkward encounters with him, she'd begged off; which he agreed was for the best. Seeing her today would merely amplify his already dire mood.

Mike searched for Bob among the well-wishers, but couldn't locate him. Everyone else seemed to be having a blast of a time though, which was what really counted.

Mike wished he could also relax and enjoy himself. He let go of the drapes and watched them swish together again.

In the silence while the DJ switched songs, he heard male and female voices talking in the hallway outside his bedroom. There were giggles and one girl saying, "Hey, Mary, where's the friggin' bathroom? I need to powder my nose," and another one loudly protesting, "hold on then, me first. I gotta get rid of some beer!"

Occasionally the noise of the baseball game being watched in the living room filtered in through the bedroom door, along with the smell of food and cigarettes, both regular tobacco and joints.

Mike wasn't in the mood for partying; not in the least. It was still less than twenty-four hours since he'd discovered Master Slim's corpse over at the old house, and each time he shut his eyes, he could still see the dismembered bodies and the blood splattered all over the old man's living room.

***

Since yesterday Mike had been trying to convince himself that Master Slim's death was actually a coincidence (as it related to himself) and not some backfiring of the spell they'd performed, which now constituted an additional danger to any Ashleys or Brookes that he came in contact with.

However, the facts were scary:

Ashley Hunt . . . dead.

Slim Brooks aka Master Slim . . . and Dave Brooks . . . also dead. And both of them on the same night.

Okay, so yes, 'Brooks' was technically a surname and not the same as 'Brooke,' but who was to say that whatever malicious spirit was responsible for their deaths hadn't suddenly become indiscriminate in its selection of victims? Mike couldn't forget the bloody pentagram he'd seen drawn on the floor of the occultist's inner room. What if the police were wrong and the killers (assuming that, yes, they were human and not supernatural) *had* been performing some kind of demonic ritual in there?

***

There was a knock on the bedroom door. "Hey, dude, you still inside there?"

"Yeah."

The door opened and Bob stepped inside. While his bestie was holding the door open, Mike caught a flash of a girl in a red-and-yellow dress and 'fuck me' heels walking past. Bob looked back at the girl and then turned and winked at Mike. "That's Rosemary Finch. Dude, am I so gonna get laid tonight!"

Bob was wearing a dark tee-shirt with 'YEAH, DUDE!' boldly inscribed on it in white letters—Mike's birthday present to him—and jeans shorts. His blonde hair was held in place by a white sweatband. Flip-flops completed his party getup. He was eating part of a chicken and had a half-empty plastic cup of beer in his other hand. He was grinning broadly, clearing enjoying himself; but he quickly sobered when he saw the look on Mike's face.

"Hey, dude, don't tell me you're still moping on all those deaths. That's awful."

Mike sat on the edge of the bed and sighed deeply. "I can't stop thinking about them."

Bob ate some chicken and washed the bird down with beer. "Dude, I already told you that the cop lady was right with her coincidence theory. Nothing supernatural is actively killing your girlfriends. Mortika ain't dead yet, is she?"

That was the sticking point in Mike's argument. Yes, Mortika *was* still alive. Mike, distracted enough by the deaths to drive past her shop, had seen her alive and well this afternoon on his way home from work.

So if a spell hadn't killed Mortika . . . ?

"But, man, I didn't *really* date her, did I?" he told Bob.

"Mike, you 'dated' Mortika longer than you did Ashley Hunt. You hadn't even properly asked Ashley out yet. Reason this with me, dude: You knew Ashley for how long? Two days? And now she's dead. Okay, but you'd known Mortika for over a day before that, and yet she's still alive. Come on, dude, that's more than long enough for a vengeful spirit to have knocked her off too if it had planned on doing so. In this case I'd have assumed that it's first come, first served."

"Bob, you're forgetting that Mortika is a witch; maybe she reached a deal with whatever thing killed the others."

Bob finished his beer and crumpled the plastic cup. The DJ was now playing *Bounce Like Me* by 'Chill Bill' Wachowski and he raised his voice to be heard over the pounding hip-hop bass: "Hey, dude, listen to me here. You sound ridiculous and I sound ridiculous too discussing spirits and devils and magic like this, but okay, what are we gonna do now?"

Mike shrugged. "If only I had a way to summon Ashley Cummins from the grave again and ask her what's going on now."

Bob grinned. "Well, we could ask Mortika to have a look in the afterlife for us."

Mike scowled back at him. "Man, that isn't even funny to start with. And you don't think I'm gonna ask Mortika for anything, do you? She'll just assume I still wanna fuck her."

Bob grinned some more. "Maybe *you should* fuck her. It doesn't seem to have done Kirk any harm. He's out there now seducing away like he'll get an award for it. No shit, I mean the guy should have been born a dog." Bob walked over to the bedroom window, parted the drapes a little and peeked out himself.

Then suddenly he looked horrified and yelped: "Oh shit, Mike! I've got big trouble!"

"What's the matter? You look like the two dead Ashleys just gatecrashed your party."

"No, no, dude, I ain't scared of no ghosts; this is a *major* emergency. Dude, I gotta run if I still wanna get laid tonight. Kirk's just latched onto Rosemary . . . and . . . she's already giving him that smile girls give boys when they plan on spreading their legs wide."

Bob was out of there in a flash. The look of panic on his face as he went was so comical that Mike burst out laughing.

But that burst of laughter cured Mike of his blues. He noted that in his panic Bob had dropped his unfinished chicken on the floor, then, still laughing, he pulled on his sneakers and left the bedroom to join the revelry.

CHAPTER 17

Okay, okay, Mike thought as he stepped out from the rear of the house into the fast-setting dusk, *to keep my sanity, I'm gonna assume that the four deaths after the ritual really were coincidences and that any girls I chat up now are safe. But . . . Bob's suggestion isn't that bad after all—I actually can ask Mortika to raise up Ashley Cummins for me. Strictly as a professional contract of course. I'll make it one hundred percent clear to her that I'm hiring just her services, not her body . . . I've no interest in romancing her*

He quickly found himself lost in the crush of gyrating bodies. He realized he was hungry, pushed through the dancers to one of the barbeque grills and got himself a plate of chicken. He stood by the barbeque grill, scanning the crowd for Bob.

"Hey, Mike!"

It was Jane. She was slightly drunk and had been dancing with another slightly drunk girl when she'd sighted him. She flung her arms around him. "Hi there! I was wondering where you'd got to?"

Mike quickly disentangled himself from her. "I'm looking for Bobby. Have you seen him?"

She pointed towards the far end of the yard. "Over there, I think."

"Thanks." After picking out a beer from an iced cooler of them, Mike hurried off through the dancers.

Bob, Kirk and Rosemary Finch were standing under a tree at the end of the yard, where the music wasn't so loud. Bob was still trying to 'rescue' Rosemary Finch from Kirk's 'clutches'—Kirk had his arm draped over her shoulders—and understandably had the look of a desperate man.

Mike sighed, wondering how many of the women here at the party Kirk had already slept with. He and Bob had agreed never to accept Kirk's leftovers though, so if Rosemary went off with Kirk, that would be it as far she and Bob was concerned.

"Hey, listen to this one," Kirk was telling the girl, while leering at her abundant cleavage. "So, okay, if a guy beats up his girl or his wife, that's domestic violence, right? But what if she's a mermaid and her lower half's a fish? Does that make it domestic fry-olence?"

Kirk burst out laughing while Rosemary Finch looked suitably impressed. Girls always looked impressed when Kirk told a joke, no matter how lame it was.

Bob just rolled his eyes.

"Hey, just the man I wanted to see," Kirk said on noticing Mike. "Bob said you were asleep." He gestured back at the dancers and the DJ. "I don't know how you managed sleeping through all this noise." He winked. "Lotsa hot bitches, right?"

Mike sighed. "Where's your new girl Mortika? I don't see her anywhere?"

"Oh, she's probably out casting a spell on someone." Then Kirk smirked. "Hey, dude don't be sore. You can't blame her for choosing me over you."

"I'm not sore, man. I'm no longer sore about Jane either."

On hearing about Mortika, Rosemary lost a little of her enthusiasm. She wiggled out from under Kirk's arm and stepped closer to Bob.

Kirk hardly seemed to notice the girl's desertion. "Hey, man, I wanna introduce you to some people," he told Mike.

"Just a moment," Mike said and then dragged Bob away to one side.

"Thanks for the assist," Bob said, with a glance back at Rosemary, who was still making no attempt to return to Kirk's side.

"You ain't out of the woods yet, dude," Mike said. "Though I don't know why you're so stuck on her. You're the birthday boy; there's lots of young women here to choose from."

"Two words, dude—her chest."

Mike nodded. Rosemary Finch was very well-endowed; her completely natural D-cup breasts were practically bursting out of her red and yellow dress.

"Listen," Mike went on, "from the frustrated look on her face, I'd say Rosemary still wants to fuck Kirk, but is worried about his girlfriend turning up unannounced and making a scene while they're in bed together. So you gotta get in there first while she still can't make up her mind what to do."

"Dude, how'm I supposed to do that?"

"It's your party, man. Remember, out of sight is usually out of mind. Just keep her far away from Kirk and he'll soon find himself another girl-toy to play with. Let Rosemary call you 'Kirk' in bed if she likes."

Bob shrugged. "Guess it's worth a try. I'll feel like the world's greatest loser tomorrow if I don't hold those great tits in my hands tonight."

Bob walked back over to Rosemary and whispered something in her ear. She nodded enthusiastically and walked off with him.

Mike grinned. *Maybe I was wrong about her and she really has lost her interest in Kirk since hearing about Mortika.*

"Hey, Mike."

He turned back to Kirk. "Yeah, man, you said you want to introduce me to someone?"

"Not someone. Two young women who I'm certain will be great for you."

"Great for me?" This was a first. Kirk never set up his friends with girls. "What's this about? It's a trick, right?"

Kirk shook his head. In the fading daylight; there was something hostile about his face. Mike thought he looked very angry about something, but was doing his best to conceal it. His anger couldn't be over Rosemary though. She wasn't the prettiest girl at the party. There were lots of other pretty girls around, several of whom were glancing their way now that Rosemary was out of the picture, clearly waiting till Kirk was alone again before they walked over to seduce him.

Wish I could be so lucky, Mike thought. *And here I am, needing to ask each girl I meet if her name is Brooke or Ashley.*

"These two girls are my cousins," Kirk explained, while grabbing Mike by the elbow and steering him through the crush of dancers. They're twins and don't have a date and so I thought I'd introduce you to them."

"Your cousins? Hey, man, there's no need for that. I can find my own women."

"Oh, it's the least I can do," Kirk replied. "Seeing as I've recently stolen two beautiful young women from you, it's only right if I repay you by introducing you to these two beautiful young women."

The malice in Kirk's voice was palpable; there was clearly more to this than him wanting to amends for his earlier betrayals of their friendship. Mike wanted to protest further that he wasn't interested, but Kirk's grip on his arm was viselike. And besides, they'd already arrived at where they were headed.

A seating area had been arranged beneath the trees on the opposite side of the backyard from where they'd earlier been standing; groups of foldup chairs around tables with parasols stuck through them. It was on one of these tables that the sad remnants of the 'BOB IS 28!' cake cut earlier in the day sat. A few people sat around the tables, sipping soft drinks and beers and watching the dancers.

Kirk led Bob to one of the farther tables, where two identical blondes sat side by side drinking Bud Lights. One of them wore a white dress, the other a black one. Yes, they were undeniably beautiful, on a par with the prettiest amongst the dancing throng. However, as he and Kirk got nearer to the pair, Mike sensed there was something odd about them, but he couldn't tell what it was.

He was filled with a sense of regret that two girls this beautiful weren't for him.

"And now, man," Kirk said, in an impresario's voice that somehow still dripped with malice, "let me introduce you to my gorgeous cousins Brooke and Ashley Lawrence . . . aka 'Brash.'

What? Mike couldn't help gaping at the twins. How could Kirk have known? Had Bob told him? But no, Bob was a true friend, he would never let out a secret like that to anyone, let alone the traitorous Kirk.

So this is just a coincidence then? What? Is there a 'Brooke and Ashley' tree planted somewhere around here?

The twins were smiling at him and he had to say something. Laughing loudly, Kirk had already walked off.

"Hi, I'm Mike," he said. "Pleased to meet you both."

And it was then, when one girl extended her right hand to shake him, and the other her left hand, that Mike noticed the strangeness about them.

Brooke and Ashley Lawrence were conjoined twins. Siamese twins. As far as he could see, their bodies were fused into a single wide expanse of torso, leaving each of them with a full set of legs and breasts, but with only one arm each. The girls weren't wearing two separate dresses, but a single one, its right side white, its left side black. Similarly, their fingernails were painted to match their clothes. He was standing too close to the table to notice if their shoes also matched the same split color scheme.

"You're . . . you're . . . you're . . ." he gasped. He'd not been this shocked in . . . in . . . like forever.

"Yes, we're stuck together," the girl on the left (which was actually their own right side) sighed. "Hope that isn't a problem?"

"No . . . no problem at all," Mike lied. "But I'm incredibly surprised." Here too the music was much less louder than it was nearer the house, so they didn't need to shout at each other to be heard.

"We're completely normal young women," the girl on the right said. "We're just a little unusual, that's all."

"Kirk didn't tell me you were conjoined twins," Mike explained.

"Kirk's a jerk."

"He treats us like the family freak show. You heard how he made his voice sound like he was making an announcement in a circus. He does that to us all the time."

"We hate it!"

"Yes we do!"

"We only tolerate it 'cos he's family. But one of these days he's really gonna go too far."

"And then . . ."

Though not identical, their voices were eerily similar; clearly the product of each girl patterning her speech rhythms and word choices on the other. Otherwise, they both spoke with a gravelly midrange drawl that was very pleasant to listen to.

"Eddie's okay though," the 'right' girl said. "But Kirk? Kirk's a crappy piece of work."

"A complete dickhead," the 'left' girl agreed.

Mike found himself warming to the twins. Anyone who thought Kirk was a dickhead was okay with him.

And besides they were a Brooke and an Ashley combined in one. He sat down, and set down his plate of chicken and his can of beer (both of which he'd forgotten he was carrying) on the table, and grinned at the twins who were both smiling expectantly at him.

"Hey, so which of you ladies is which?" he asked. "Which of you is Ashley, which one Brooke?"

"I'm Brooke and she's Ashley," the girl on the left said while pointing first at herself and then at her twin.

"It's easiest to remember if you think of us as 'Brash,' from B . . . R . . . Brooke and A . . . S . . . H . . . Ashley," her sister explained.

Mike nodded. "Cool, I got it." He too pointed from one to the other. "Brooke and Ashley."

"We're not really *brash* though," Ashley said. "But we're very bold 'cos otherwise we'd have to live as underdogs, with people treating us like circus freaks."

"Yeah, and we don't want anyone either pitying us or looking down on us," Brooke agreed. "As kids we were homeschooled for a while, but we told our parents we wanted to attend high school like everyone else. So they let us."

"We didn't let anyone—boys or girls—bully us."

Mike nodded. There was something about the pair that spoke of a huge determination to make the most of the huge lemon defective genetics had handed them.

"We can't be separated—we share too many organs."

"I can just imagine what that's like," Mike said.

Mike didn't know if it was the beer in his system, or the fact that both girls were so pretty, or simply the fact that they were a Brooke and an Ashley, but he really liked the pair.

"What do you girls do for a living?" he asked.

"We design websites. It's a good job and it also means we can work at home," Brooke explained. "We don't mind going out, but getting stared at all the time at the mall gets very tiring."

"Besides, it's easier to just order groceries online."

Mike nodded and got to his feet.

"Hey, where you going?" Ashley immediately asked.

"Yeah, we're not boring you, are we?"

"No, no," Mike said. "My beer's empty, I just wanna get another one." He gestured to their own drinks. "You girls want more beers too?"

Ashley shook her head. "Nah, I'm driving."

Mike looked at Brooke. "You?"

She laughed and ran her finger down the seam that separated the black and white sections of their dress. "You don't get it, do you, man? If *I* drink, *she* drinks. Our circulatory systems are linked. It's one of the reasons why the doctors can't separate us."

Mike nodded. "I'm gonna have to get used this. Give me a few minutes, and I'll be right back."

"Hey, make sure you do come back," Ashley said. "I'd like a sandwich, please."

"Yeah, we like you," Brooke agreed. "Bring me some barbeque and coleslaw."

Ashley Cummins must be laughing her head off in the afterlife, Mike thought as he crossed through the dancers to where the food and drinks were.

He also thought he saw where this meeting with 'Brash' was leading: The twins clearly liked him and saw him as a potential boyfriend; well, for at least one of them.

Okay, so weirdness aside, I really like those two girls too. But only as friends. There is no way under heaven—absolutely no fucking way at all—that I'm dating one of a set of Siamese twins.

From a vantage point near one of the barbeque grills, he looked back across the yard. Brooke and Ashley's table was obscured by the dancers.

The simplest way out of this is for me to make a run for it now that they can't see me—leave the party, go off and get drunk at Rudy's Truck Stop and see if they've any new pretty waitresses there. Then he smacked a hand against his head. *Oh yeah, that's right, I can't go to Rudy's. At the moment I'm persona non grata there. Rudy is still mad at me—he still blames me for Linda's death.*

Mike got a tray of barbequed meat, a large sandwich, some soft drinks for the twins and two beers for himself. Then he headed back through the dancers to sit with 'Brash' again. And then he got down to knowing the girls better.

***

The Lawrence twins lived down in Taunton, the town that abutted on the southern part of Raynham.

Brooke was the bolder of the pair, the one who initiated most of their schemes. Ashley had ideas too, but she generally deferred to her twin's interpretation of any situation. Seeing as where one of them went, the other had no choice but to follow, and also that they only had one set of hands between them, they always needed to reach an agreement on any plans before carrying them out. Which extended from mundane tasks like cooking and washing up, to intimate matters like using the toilet and changing tampons, and included such important matters as dating.

They were thinking of getting some pets, but hadn't yet agreed on which they preferred—dogs or cats?

Though Ashley seemed calmer than Brooke, she had more of a temper.

Ashley was the main driver for their car, an old Ford convertible which had a bench seat that accommodated them both. Ashley operated the gas pedal and the clutch and brake. Brooke wished she could do that, but she was on the wrong side of their body; she helped out with the steering wheel and also manipulated the vehicle's gearshift and blinkers.

***

"Hey, you girls wanna dance?" Mike asked after a while.

"Hell yeah, we thought you'd never ask," Brooke said, with Ashley nodding enthusiastically.

The girls got to their feet. After noting that he'd been right—their shoes matched their clothes; white on the right and black on the left—Mike led them a short distance from their table and they began shaking themselves to the music too.

The twins were good dancers. They drew a few stares from the other partygoers, though most people simply assumed they were two girls dancing close side by side.

Mike didn't care what anyone thought. The twins were happy and so was he. This was the happiest he'd felt all week.

***

The twins left at midnight, stepping soberly through the mostly inebriated crowd.

As he walked the girls to their vehicle, Mike looked around for Bob but couldn't find him. He didn't see Kirk anywhere either.

Mike did see Kirk's younger brother Eddie though. Eddie was dancing with Bob's sister Karen, a bespectacled brunette who looked even more nerdy than himself. Nerdiness aside though, both of them were tipsy and giggling loudly.

"Hey, I love your dress!" Karen shouted at the Lawrence twins over the loud music. "Fucking great color scheme!"

"You guys seen Bob!?" Mike shouted back at her and Eddie.

"And where's Kirk vanished to!?" Brooke also shouted.

"And with whom!?" Ashley shouted. "Which girls are missing from the party now? Who's gone off to be initiated into the woes of sluthood!?"

"K-Kirk left!" Eddie shouted. "I think he went to see Mortika!"

Karen pointed. "Bobby's in the house!" she shouted. "But don't you dare disturb him; he was kissing Rosie when they left!" She made a gesture of grabbing her breasts. "You know, Rosie with the huge boobs!?" She giggled. "I think they went to do it!"

Mike nodded and he and the twins left the pair, walking around the side of the house to the twins' car.

"Hey, tonight was really nice," Brooke said once both girls were seated in the Ford convertible. Out here the sound was normal again, the loudspeaker noise a rumble on the other side of the bungalow. "We really enjoyed being with you, Mike."

"Call us soon," Ashley said. "You've got both our numbers. Doesn't matter which of us you call, the other one won't be far away."

Mike laughed at that, replied, "Sure thing," and the girls drove off.

Mike watched the conjoined pair leave with mixed emotions.

Well, they're most definitely nice and interesting young women, he thought calmly. *But, hey!—there is simply no way that I'm going anywhere with those two.*

CHAPTER 18

It was several days later before Mike really thought about the Lawrence twins again. Now that Bob's birthday party was over, his life fell back into its normal routine of work, work and more work.

For Bob, sex with Rosemary Finch proved to be just a one night stand. Though sleeping with Bob on the night of his birthday party was an enormous ego boost for her, in the cold light of the morning after, she wasn't about to date him. Rosemary's parents were too rich for her to date a lowly Walmart overnight stocker.

So that was that.

Bob didn't care. "Ah, dude," he gushed to Mike on Sunday morning. "Thanks for the 'Dude' tee shirt, but, dude, those tits of hers were the only birthday present I really needed. Waking up with my head pillowed on them . . . oh dude! Hope she comes again next year!"

"You did use condoms, right?"

Bob scratched his head. "I don't remember; I'm gonna have to ask Rosemary. But, shit, she likely won't remember either; she was even drunker than I was. But, wow, dude, I really like her—she puts her boobs into everything she does."

"Forget her chest for a moment, consider the state of her belly; it might soon be inflating. Her folks are gonna have a fit if you've knocked her up."

Bob sighed dreamily. "But just imagine if she is pregs and she wants to keep it . . . then I could come home to those divine boobies every morning . . . And you know how pregnancy makes a woman's breasts grow even bigger . . . Oh, heaven."

Mike left him to dream. There was no chance in hell of him ever marrying Rosemary Finch. If she was pregnant from last night, her stuck-up folks were certain to talk her into aborting the baby.

***

And so the week passed. Monday, Tuesday, Wednesday . . . during which time Mike toyed with the idea of joining several online dating clubs, but somehow never took the plunge.

He still avoided visiting the McDonald's opposite Mortika's shop after work, buying his takeaways at the franchise's restaurant up on Broadway instead. Avoiding Mortika was fast becoming a habit.

But then on Thursday morning, he suddenly decided to call 'Brash.'

Mike was at work when the impulse to call the twins hit him. He was seated in one of the electronics department's offices and was reviewing the inventory for 3M, a large gym down the highway that was ordering a new audio system.

3M (or Mike's Muscle Mall) wanted to completely rewire their two-story building so as to pipe central audio all through it, and they wanted the Cashstretch audio engineers to handle the installation for them.

Mike was overseeing the project.

Taking a break from rechecking his estimate of how many loudspeakers and how many feet of audio cable were required, he looked up the twins' phone numbers on his cellphone, and then debated which one of them to call. Finally though, he realized it was a dumb concern; whichever twin he called had her twin sister right beside her. And once they knew he was the one on the line, they were certain to put the phone on speakerphone to take the call. Which of course made him also wonder why they'd bothered to give him both of their numbers, or why they even had separate cellphones to begin with. It wasn't as if they would ever be in two different places at once.

Ashley's name was before Brooke's in the contacts list, so he called her.

"Hi, handsome," Ashley gushed into the phone on picking up, "we thought you weren't gonna call us." At least Mike assumed it was Ashley speaking and not Brooke, but he no longer remembered what each girl sounded like.

"Yeah, sometimes men are turned off by us," Brooke said, confirming his suspicion that they'd put the phone on speakerphone. "I guess that's 'cos we're a lot of woman to deal with."

"Yeah, twice as much as the average girl. But that's a plus!"

"How are you doing? Have you and Bob gotten your backyard cleaned up yet?"

Mike laughed at the question. "Yeah, it's mostly clean now. Bob's sister Karen and a few friends helped us pick up the garbage on Sunday. So, how've you girls been?"

"Oh, we're fine. Webpage design isn't really that exciting. Once you've built one website you've built 'em all."

"Yeah, it's just the graphics that are different. But it pays the rent."

"Okay," Mike said cautiously, "to alleviate the boredom a little, would you girls like to go out tonight?"

An excited voice (Mike had now given up trying to figure out which sister was speaking): "Yeah, we'd love to!"

A questioning, cautious voice: "But where are we gonna go? Where d'you have in mind, Mike?"

Mike didn't have anywhere in mind. He'd not really intended on asking them out; he'd just wanted to say hello and chat a bit. But something about their voices attracted him to them and now he'd taken the plunge. He was just realizing the implication of what he'd said: *I've asked them out on a date, and this isn't a normal situation where you take one sister out and not the other—with these two it's a package deal or nothing. I'm dating two girls and if it works out I'll have two girlfriends, not one.*

"Mike, you still there?"

"Hey, don't you dare hang up on us now!"

"Yeah, I'm here. I'm simply trying to work out where to go."

"Hey, let's go to Rudy's."

"Oh heck, not Rudy's. C'mon, Brooke, those greasy fries of his are utterly disgusting."

"They don't taste so bad after a few beers. And I love the tunes on that ancient jukebox they have there."

"Oh, okay, and besides, we'll be killing two birds with one stone anyway."

"Hey," Mike said, "I thought you girls didn't drink."

"We don't when *we're* driving. But *you'll* be driving tonight, right?"

Mike nodded. "Yeah, that's right. What do you mean by 'you'll be killing two birds with one stone?'"

"Oh, we're designing a website for Rudy's Truck Stop and we want to take a few shots of the interior of the place when it's packed with customers."

"Yeah, we keep asking Rudy to send us photos, but all the ones he sends over are total shite. The image resolutions are crap—not even good enough for thumbnails."

"We've no idea why the old guy won't simply invest in a decent cellphone."

Mike laughed. "Okay, I get it." He sneaked a peek out through the office door to ensure he wasn't currently needed out in Electronics. "Cool, we're all set up for tonight then. Alright, I gotta get back to pretending to earn my paycheck. So, I'll pick you ladies up at 8 p.m.?"

"Yeah, that's great."

"Fantastic! We'll text you our house address. It's very easy to find."

"Yeah, we look forward to seeing you again."

Mike hung up and grinned. Tonight was sure to be quite an experience.

CHAPTER 19

Mike and the twins arrived at Rudy's Truck Stop at 9 p.m.

Even with the weekend still twenty-four hours away and last call several hours away, Rudy's boasted a good crowd, a fair percentage of whom were already quite drunk. Truckers, bikers and other road gypsies filled booths and sat at the bar, with two or three denim-clad couples swaying cheek-to-cheek on the checkered dance floor area, while the stereo blared out *Loveless Song*, by Slain Jane:

"Yeah, I love you,
I definitely do love you, honey,
Though I sure as hell don't know why.
You treat me like a dog,
A pet-shelter mongrel not a pampered Chihuahua,
And that really makes me cry . . ."

Tonight the twins were dressed in a short black leather skirt and an all-pink tee-shirt with two head holes. Mike now had a better idea of their shared anatomy: their hip bones were apparently fused, because though visibly separate, their 'inner' legs tended to move as one.

Both twins wore their blonde hair pulled back in ponytails; and both wore bright red lipstick and lots of blue eyeshadow. They wore identical brown thong sandals and carried matching brown purses.

The girls caused a bit of a stir when they entered the truck stop, pushing in through the glass double door with confidence like they owned the drinking establishment. All the heads in the place turned to look at the strange sight. But after a few double takes, those patrons who were already drunk seemed to think the alcohol in their systems was making them see double and ignored the twins, while those who weren't yet drunk apparently decided they needed more alcohol in their bloodstreams to help them ignore the twins.

Mike and the girls walked over to the bar. There were no free stools available, so they stood at the end of the bar, near an empty booth.

Rudy walked over. He smiled at the twins and frowned at Mike. "Hey, don't you dare get these two killed," he growled. "At least not before my website's finished."

"What's he talking about?" Brooke asked Mike.

"Sonofabitch got my best waitress killed," Rudy told the girls. "My best waitress ever. By all rights, I shouldn't even let him drink here anymore."

"Hey, it wasn't my fault," Mike protested to the hulking bartender. He wasn't about making an issue of the false accusation though. Rudy was too big and looked too mean to argue with. Hell, even the bikers didn't dare piss the big guy off.

"Yeah, it warn't 'is fault, Ruud," the drunk beside them agreed. "Ways I heards it—some drunken guy ran a red light and . . . Lin . . . Lin . . . Linda . . . yeah, thas her nime . . . well, she warn't wearing no seatbelt."

Mike was grateful to the guy and decided not to correct the mistakes in his statement.

"Yeah, whatever," Ruby growled, banging a brawny hirsute arm down on the counter while simultaneously shooting Mike a black look. "Just take care of these two twin cuties or I'll ban ya from drinking anywhere for life!" Then he grinned at the twins. "How's my website comin' along, girls?"

"Almost done," Brooke said brightly. "We should have you online by next Tuesday, but the photos you sent us aren't good enough to use."

"They ain't?" Rudy enquired in some perplexity.

Ashley shook her head. "Nah, bad lighting."

She was being *very* kind. The twins had shown Mike the photos Rudy had sent them. They were practically anti-advertisements for his business: bad camera angles, poor focus, more darkness than light and to top that off, across the board the image quality was so low, the pictures all seemed to contain giant pixels. Rudy must need glasses. Not that Mike dared point that out to him.

"But not to worry," Brooke grinned, "we brought along our trusty digital camera. We'll get some good shots tonight."

Rudy grinned back, showing dirty yellow teeth. "So, girls, now what'll you be drinkin'?"

"Three beers," Ashley said.

Rudy did the math in his head, then stared coldly at Mike. "No beers for you, not so long as you've got these girls in your darn truck."

Mike didn't say a word. Rudy struck him as being irate enough and irrational enough to knock his teeth in if he dared protest.

Brooke came to his rescue: "Oh, come on, Rudy, lighten up. Since Mike's driving, we'll keep a watch on his alcohol consumption. We'll stop him on three bottles."

Rudy frowned, then acquiesced. "Okay, girls, but only 'cos you two say so."

They got their first round of beers, secured the booth near the corner of the bar, and started drinking.

The stereo switched to playing Slain Jane's *Antidote For God.*

"Oh, goody, I just love this song," Ashley said.

"Phooey, I just hate it," Brooke instantly countered.

***

Mike once more found Brooke and Ashley Lawrence to be fun company. This bothered him a little; he'd have preferred them to be neurotic bitches with all sorts of personality disorders, then he would have a very clear-cut reason for not seeing them again. He did feel certain that if he hung around them both long enough (well, he couldn't exactly separate them, could he?) the cracks in their well-polished exterior would begin to show.

And (he realized with a sudden surge of terror racing through him) *I need those cracks to show up quickly, before I get too deeply involved with these two permanently-associated young women.*

Because, for one thing, what the hell did one do when it came to having sex with them? Because, except this date proved to be a major train wreck, that was certainly where tonight was heading. He sensed an intense seductive vibe coming from the twins; they rubbed up against him every chance they got and kept smiling coyly and stroking his hands.

"So, man, what's been happening at your job lately?" Ashley asked him while stroking his hand. And if there had been any doubt before about him getting laid tonight it was swept aside when two sets of bare feet began playing footsie with him under the table, a pair sneaking up each trouser leg. He tried to keep a straight face while replying the twins, but it was very hard because of the erection he suddenly got.

"N-n-not m-much," he said. "B-b-but I'm overseeing a contract to outfit a gym down our road—Route 44—with a new sound system. We're taking the old one out and putting in a completely new system, wiring and all."

"Which gym is that?" Brooke said. "I don't remember seeing any gyms down that way."

"It's called 3M . . . or Mike's Muscle Mall if you prefer," Mike replied. "You know—the Rossi place; the owner and his boyfriend were murdered in their beds. Chopped completely to pieces. It was major news headlines last summer."

"Oh yes, I remember now," Ashley said. "Their neighbor Steve-O—the guy living in the house opposite—he was killed too. All on the same night."

"Yeah, now I remember that story too," Brooke said with a look of disgust. "That guy—the neighbor—was said to be making snuff movies in his basement and some other gangsters killed him and his partners and his girlfriend."

"Yeah, but the police never found any clues as to the killers," Mike agreed.

"Oh, so the guy's gym is still open?" Ashley asked. "It didn't close down after he died?"

Mike shook his head. Before replying he signaled a waitress to bring them fresh beers. "Oh, it shut down for a few months," he told the twins. "But then Mike Rossi's sister Angela—she married his boyfriend's brother—"

"Wow, talk about keeping it in the family."

Mike laughed. "Well, yeah, they did keep it in the family. So anyway, Angela married the boyfriend's brother Carl and they've decided to reopen the place. But apparently while the building was shut down, rats and water leakage fucked up the audio system big-time so they need to completely replace it." He shrugged. "Normally, they'd hire a contractor, but Angela handles some of Cashstretch's legal affairs, so we agreed to do it for her. She and Carl also bought Steve-O's club down in Taunton—the Clip nightclub. We're fixing that one up also."

Possibly due to the dark nature of what they'd just discussed, the twins had thankfully now stopped caressing Mike with their feet, and his penis had softened again. However, he was still very distracted by them. Once more he was dismayed by how easily he forgot that they were permanently attached to each other, and had just two arms instead of four. Their single tee-shirt should at least have reinforced this peculiar oddity in his mind, but he found himself overlooking it in favor of looking at their breasts, which though small, were nicely formed, four sweet mounds in a row, each decorated with a large nipple. They weren't wearing a bra.

He felt his erection returning and realized he'd been paying too much attention to their breasts. He looked back up at their faces. They'd been whispering something to themselves, but now both turned and winked at him simultaneously. From their eyes, he got the impression that Brooke and Ashley knew he'd been studying their shared cleavage and that they very much approved of his doing so.

This won't do at all, he told himself as the loud music and smell of booze and food and clinking of cutlery on plates and bottles and glasses, and chattering voices and sweaty dancing bodies nearby conspired against him, urging him to just relax and give in to the twins' inviting smiles and their pleasant presence. *I need to keep a clear focus here; being with these two is only going to complicate my life in a major way!*

Their conversation now turned to mundane things: Politics (Brooke was a republican and Ashley a democrat; so they never voted as they'd merely wind up neutralizing one another.); movies (both girls loved chick flicks and wanted to be actresses, though they understood that for special women like themselves, good romantic roles would necessarily be limited); fashion (being two-in-one meant you had to have your clothes hand-tailored, and then you also had to be able to find shoes and handbags in matching colors to your clothes; and music (they both liked EDM; Ashley could sing but Brooke couldn't, though she had a much better memory for song names and lyrics than her sister did; and both of them loved 'Chill Bill' Wachowski); family (their parents were both alive and still married and lived in Taunton with their teenaged brother. They'd grown up there, but had attended college in Springfield).

The evening rolled on nicely, though the proprietor Rudy kept to his word and policed Mike's alcohol intake, while he let the twins drink all they wanted.

They all had the obligatory truck stop cheeseburgers and greasy fries and when the crowd was at their rowdiest, and before the twins got too tipsy to focus their camera, the girls left the booth and took the photos of the truck stop that they needed to complete the website. That was weird to watch, as they kept shifting the camera from one head to the other, to agree on what exactly they were shooting.

And then, after Mike paid the bar tab, it was time to leave for home.

CHAPTER 20

All the doorways in the twins' bungalow were wider than usual and were designed saloon style, to split in the middle.

Mike followed the two staggering and giggling young women into their living room. Earlier, when he'd stopped by to pick them up, he'd expected their armchairs to be proportionately wider too, but the twins didn't have any armchairs; instead they had three couches.

"And now . . . now that we've brought you to our lair," Brooke said in sexily slurred tones, as she and Ashley whirled around and around like drunken dancers. "Now it's time for us to have our wicked way with you, baby!"

By now Mike was more than ready for them to have their wicked way with him. Ashley, who'd naturally been seated nearer to him on the pickup truck's front bench seat on the drive down from Rudy's, had been massaging his crotch all the way. She'd almost made him ejaculate in his pants.

The twins got a bottle of wine from the kitchen and then, giggling madly, they pulled Mike into the bedroom with them.

They had a large bed onto which they pushed Mike. Then, while pulling off his own clothes, he watched them get undressed too.

Though swaying drunkenly, this was easy enough for them to do; after kicking their sandals off and discarding their handbags on the floor, the tee shirt went up over their heads and the skirt went down to their ankles. Panty-wise, they wore some kind of double-thong that was quickly discarded.

"So, do you like what you'll be getting?" Brooke asked coyly, with Ashley's identical face giggling.

Mike nodded. "I couldn't ask for anything better than the two of you." The fusion of their bodies seemed natural. The continuing expanse of flesh between hip and shoulder where arm otherwise should have been looked too ordinary to dispute. Their little breasts were perfectly shaped and thrusting, their nipples aggressively stiff and calling for his hands to caress them and his lips to suck on them

And then the girls advanced on Mike. Mike relaxed and let them have him.

The sex was more normal than he'd expected it to be; with lots of kissing and caressing; two girls, one body.

Ashley seemed to be the more passionate of the sisters. Brooke seemed distracted, either because she was more focused on playing with his erection or because she was simply too drunk.

The fact that they looked exactly alike negated the question of their varying degree of libido.

The sixty-nine was odd though. The girls quickly initiated him into what they called 'cross-body cunnilingus.' Simply put, this involved him being fellated by Brooke while he licked Ashley's clitoris, and then being fellated by Ashley while he did the same to her sister.

Then, deciding to work from left to right, Mike slipped a condom on, parted Brooke's legs and inserted himself into her. He thrust slowly into her while playing with Ashley's crotch. He went slowly because he didn't know how much longer he was going to last. The alcohol he'd drunk was delaying his ejaculation slightly, but still, he was very close to coming and he felt he was expected to get both twins off first.

Brooke gazed up at him with lustful eyes. and stroked his back with her hand, while Ashley thrust up her crotch, grabbed his hand and dipped his fingers into her sex.

Mike was both surprised and gratified when Ashley suddenly yelped, "Oh, shit, yes—I'm coming!"

Mike slowed down his thrusts into her sister, and concentrated on getting Ashley off with his fingers.

After a while, she grinned at him. "I'm fine, you can take care of Brooke now. But my pussy is here for you if you don't come inside of her."

Mike concentrated on Brooke, who seemed to be falling asleep. Even though the girls shared their bloodstream, alcohol clearly affected them differently, with Brooke getting the worst of it, tonight at least.

But then, as Ashley relaxed with a broad grin on her face, Brooke suddenly dug her fingernails deep into Mike's back.

"Shit!" he yelped from the pain.

"Yeah, fuck her hard like that," Ashley said, reaching across and clawing his back with her own fingernails also.

Mike thrust very hard and very deep into Brooke, the pain from the girls' raking fingernails providing him with encouragement to hurt her like she was hurting him. But instead of whimpering in pain, Brooke just spread her legs wider to accommodate his penis better.

"Oh, my fucking God, yes, yes yesssss!" she moaned as her climax hit her.

Mike felt her sex tighten around his; it felt like a hand squeezing his penis. The feeling was irresistible and he let himself go.

For a while, he lay panting on the two girls, and then Brooke gently pushed him aside. Mike lay on Brooke's right, still panting; trying to make proper sense of what had just happened.

Okay, now that was wonderful, he thought, finding Brooke's fingers and locking his with them. *Really great.* His back hurt from the scratching, but the pain was tranquilized by the pleasure.

"Ah, that was really great," Brooke gasped, smiling first at him and then at her sister.

"Yeah, it was," Ashley agreed in a dreamy voice.

"I really enjoyed it," Brooke said.

"Ha, ha—but I enjoyed it more than you did," Ashley said.

"No, you didn't."

"Yes, I did. I felt true ecstasy—just the touch of his fingers . . ."

Feeling satisfied that both sisters were satisfied, Mike had been slipping off to dreamland. But he suddenly realized that there was something unpleasant in the tone of the sisters' voices:

"Well, he came in me, not in you."

"He didn't come *in you*, Brookey, he came in a condom!"

"Sore loser! You know exactly what I mean!"

"So what? That's just because you're a greedy bitch, Brooke. I can tell that he prefers me to you."

"That's a lie!"

"No it isn't!"

Mike jerked awake again. This wasn't some casual banter they were having; they were dead serious about what they were saying. What was weirdest of all was that they were acting as if he wasn't even lying next to them.

Next, Brooke jerked her fingers away from his and the twins sat up on the bed. They moved their body across to Ashley's side of the bed, flung their legs over its edge there, and sat there facing their extra-wide dresser mirror. They now resumed their argument:

"Listen, bitch," Ashley said. "I'm tired of this shite of yours. Each time we fuck a guy, you try to take all the credit for getting him off. There's two of us in this body, remember?"

"That's because you're such a pussy, pussy! Weren't for me taking the initiative, we'd never get laid. Don't you ever forget that!"

At first the twins appeared to be speaking to the mirror. But then, Mike understood what was going on. It was simple enough really: Because their heads were so close together, the girls couldn't comfortably turn them to stare at each other, so raging at one another in the mirror was the best compromise.

Okay, so I was searching for cracks in their personality and . . . wow, this is a huge one. How the hell can they argue like this . . . about me . . . with me still in the room? Watching them was horrifying, like seeing their commendable self-sufficiency mutate into narcissistic neurosis.

It was odd too, how, now that they were enraged, their prior drunkenness seemed to have vanished. *What's going on here? Were they just faking being sloshed so as to get me into bed?*

"Ha ha, so you say!" Ashley raged. "You're forgetting that if it wasn't for me, there's at least thrice you'd have gotten us raped and possibly killed."

"That's a lie—take that back! It was just the one time!"

"Hey, girls, calm down," Mike said. "Please, stop fighting."

The twins twisted around slightly to look at him.

"Shut up, Mike, you don't know anything about this," Brooke said calmly.

"No, you don't know jack, so keep out of it," Ashley quickly agreed. "This is between me and this dumb bitch here."

"She has been carrying on like this our entire life!"

"Yes she has! She looks like my reflection—damn wannabe!"

"Oh, you just wish you looked this good. You're dying to be me, aren't you?"

"See what I mean, Mike? She always thinks she's better than me!"

"Thinks she has to have more than me."

"But she's wrong!"

"He likes me more!"

"No, stupid, Mike likes me more! A whole lot more than he'll ever like you!"

Mike thought he was going crazy. Two identical faces, two near-identical voices; growling so fast at each other—while staring at him, so it appeared that he and not themselves was the focus of their duplicate anger—speaking so fast that their voices seemed to merge till he wasn't certain which of them was speaking. Now they really sounded like their nickname 'Brash.'

To worsen matters, his back had begun smarting again from the orgasmic scratching the sisters had given it.

"Hahaha, you're just so deluded, aren't you, and that's just so like you. He likes me me me, not you."

"That's what I said, bitch! He loves me, not you."

The sisters turned to look at Mike. "Which of us do you like better!?"

"Yeah, tell us the truth!"

Mike sighed. "Brooke, Ashley, I like both of you equally."

"Stop lying, Mike. You can't like *her*, 'cos she's a bitch!

"Yes, she is a lying bitch, and I really hate her. So if you truly like me like you claim, how can you also like a lying bitch that I hate!"

Mike got off the bed and began gathering his clothes from the floor.

The twins regarded him with surprise. "Hey, where you goin', Mike?" Ashley asked.

Mike was already pulling on his pants. "Home, where else? You two are going to drive me crazy."

For a moment it looked as if the Lawrence sisters would calm down again, but then Brooke shouted, "See what you've done, sis!? You're making him leave now!"

"No, I'm not!" Ashley yelled. "This is your damn fault!"

And just like that, once again seeming to forget that Mike was in the room with them, the conjoined pair returned their attention back to the mirror and resumed their argument:

"This happens every time. We find a great guy and you conspire to drive him away!"

"Conspire? Are you nuts? Conspire with who? There's only the two of us sharing this stupid body!"

Then there was a blubbery sound. "Hey, hey, bitch, don't you dare start weeping on me! I'm sure as hell not putting up with that tonight!"

Mike was sitting on the bed and pulling on his sneakers. He looked back at the twins. Brooke still looked enraged, but Ashley was crying. She was really weeping too, with tears spilling down her cheeks.

Yeah, she's still drunk, Mike decided. *Those are drunken tears; now her voice is slurring again.*

"I don't get it, Brooke! Why do you always have to be so nasty to me? Huh, what did I ever do to you? I think I'm falling for Mike and here you go again . . . You go and drive him away!"

"Shit! Not again. I told you there's no such thing as love at first sight! Yes, Mike's a great guy, but we need to get to know him better!"

"We do know him better! We just fucked him!"

"That's not how I mean it, and you know that!" Brooke now began blubbing too. "Now see what you've gone and done. You're making me cry too!"

The pair were still staring at themselves in the mirror, weeping away and looking more and more miserable by the moment.

Drunken girls or not, Mike wasn't hanging around to deal with this. He pulled on his shirt but didn't bother buttoning it up. Instead, he looked around for his cellphone, remembered that he'd left it out in the living room and quickly dashed out of the bedroom before the girls noticed he was gone.

Which happened immediately he left. Apparently one of them had either looked around, or the mirror had reflected his departure from their bedroom, because they stopped crying for a few moments, and one of them moaned:

"Oh my God, no! Now he's gone, and he won't ever come back!"

And the other twin answered: "Waaaaah! No he won't. And I like him too! I really do like him!"

"You don't like him even half as much as I do!"

"Yes I do, fuck you!"

The twins resumed crying again. Much louder this time.

Mike hurriedly got out of their house.

CHAPTER 21

The next day at work, Mike received ten different apologetic text messages from Brash.

'We're really sorry, baby. We really really are.'

'Please forgive us! Call us!'

'We know we overreacted. Sorry. Pls call.'

Etc. . .

They didn't call him; he figured they were too embarrassed to talk to him on the phone.

He didn't reply their texts; nor did he call. When the text notifications began disturbing his chain of thought, he turned them off.

Each time Mike had a nice and warm thought towards the twins, he'd instantly feel a countering twinge of pain from his clawed back and decide it wasn't worth it.

Okay, so Mike didn't really blame the twins for their weird behavior. Living in such close proximity to another person for over twenty years, and with no hope of ever being apart from them was certain to have created some weird psychological coping mechanisms, not to mention cracks in their personality.

And they had been drinking after all; so it was alright if they'd gotten a little bit riled up with each other.

But one other thing had decided him to avoid them henceforth. Last night, Brooke's nightstand had been open, and in there along with her panties, Mike had sighted a handgun, a small 'girly' revolver. Now, one thing he knew about identical twins was that they tended to do things in duplicate, meaning it was highly likely that Ashley Lawrence had a similar handgun in her own nightstand on the other side of the bed.

And alcohol and guns were always a dangerous combination. What if last night they'd switched from blaming themselves to blaming him instead?

By now I'll be perforated with holes. So no more 'Brash' for me!

***

After a while Mike was forced to put all thoughts of the Lawrence twins aside and concentrate on work. He spent half of the day overseeing the shipping of equipment to the gym down the road. There was a lot of stuff to transport, but then the 3M gym was a very large place.

Mike also met the gym's new manager, a young woman named . . . Brooke Lee.

"I was at Bob's birthday party," she told him after introductions had been made. "I saw you sitting with two blonde girls; they looked like sisters."

He nodded. He thought he recalled seeing her at the party too, but he'd been too distracted by the twins. This Brooke was tall, with long dark hair. She wasn't particularly good-looking, but wasn't unattractive either. She definitely caught—and more importantly, held—his attention . . . which was very distracting.

He stole a glance down at her left hand. She also wasn't wearing either a wedding or engagement ring.

Oh, hell no! Mike thought, on realizing where his thoughts were headed. *I've had enough of Brookes and Ashleys for a while. Well, for a few days at least. The weekend's about to start and I need to relax . . . alone . . . and undated. Plenty of time to get to know her better next week.*

So he just kept smiling politely at Brooke Lee as they went over the wiring and installation plans again.

CHAPTER 22

"It's like there's Brookes and Ashleys everywhere I turn now," Mike complained to Bob that night.

They were standing outside on their front porch. Bob was preparing to depart for another night's work of restocking Walmart's shelves.

"I know how you feel, dude," Bob said. "But it's better this way, I think. 'Cos this way, you've enough girls to make a choice from and hopefully find true love along the way. Imagine if you only knew one or two Brookes or Ashleys?"

Mike scowled. "Yeah, that wouldn't be funny in the least. My worst nightmare would be if Brash were the only two girls I knew with those names."

Bob laughed. Mike had earlier told him what had happened last night with the twins. "Listen, dude, the cool thing about dating the twins is that it's a surefire way to equalize the ratio of Brookes to Ashleys."

Bob stepped down off of the porch. Mike followed him down onto their driveway and towards the street, while protesting, "Nah, I don't think that's a wise approach at all."

"But, dude, it is—you just gotta stop thinking negative here and consider the positives of the situation."

"They're freaky."

"Looks aren't everything. Did you enjoy the sex or not?"

"Sex isn't everything."

"Dude, you're evading the question."

"No, I'm not. I really don't see how enjoying sex with them matters."

"You're *still* evading the question. Which means they must have been *fantastic* in bed."

"Bob, it's what happens before and after sex that counts. That's what you build a relationship on. Sex is just the icing on the cake."

"Wow, dude, the sex must have been fucking incredible—it's turned you into a philosopher. Whatever happened to the old 'hump them and dump them' philosophy?"

"You're mistaking me for Kirk. Now will you *please*, fucking please, stop harping on it!?"

"Okay, forget that, dude. But, you gotta admit—the twins are gorgeous; that's an argument in itself."

"They're also permanently stuck together; which completely negates their incredible beauty. And it appears that they can't stand themselves either." He frowned. "It really looked that way when they began arguing; like they've hated one another since birth."

A few people were out on the nighttime street—the elderly schoolteacher down the road was walking her dog and beyond her someone was opening up his mailbox. On their right, a car was turning out of Britton Street onto Sachem Road, while another car was heading past it in their direction. A black cat sat beneath a glowing streetlight, frozen in a pose as if waiting to be photographed and liked on social media.

"Dude, you just don't get it," Mike continued protesting. "You need to have been there and seen those girls rave at each other. Oh no, no way do I wanna be caught up in the middle of that mess again."

"If you marry them Ashley Cummins will be delighted with you."

"Ash can go to hell."

"Dude, I think she's already there. But I'm serious here—I think the twins really are a great option. Like I said, you'll be equalizing the ratio of Brookes to Ashleys in your life and for you that can only be a good thing, right? I mean, so what if they occasionally get mad at each other? All you gotta do is—"

But Mike had suddenly stopped listening to Bob.

They'd just reached the street and had turned right, with Mike intending to walk with Bob down to Broadway, which was about three hundred yards away. But now he had a sudden inkling that all wasn't well with their world. In the few seconds—less than a Microsoft minute—that they'd been out on the sidewalk, something about the night—some important and critical detail about the world around them—had changed for the worse. Tonight had suddenly become deadly for both of them.

But . . . what the hell?

Mike suddenly realized what the danger was and spun around. The black car that had been heading past the Sachem Road turnoff in their direction had suddenly sped up. The sound of its accelerating engine was what had set Mike's nerves on edge. The black car was almost upon them now, merely footsteps away, swerving up over the curb onto the sidewalk.

All Mike could do was fling himself out of the onrushing vehicle's way and hope for the best.

"BOB, JUMP!" he yelled as he leapt to the left. "BOB!"

"So, dude, I think dating the Lawrence twins is gonna do you an afterlife of good and—"

Bob was laughing when the black car hit him.

Mike had fallen hard on his side on their front lawn and really didn't see the collision. He was however conscious of a blur of dark motion streaking past him like a bullet made visible to the normal eye. One moment Bob was there out on the sidewalk and the next he wasn't; and the car that had mown him down was burning rubber, screeching out of their street onto Broadway.

Mike lay where he was for a few seconds, letting the shock of what had just happened wash over him and numbness fill his mind. Then he pulled himself up from where he'd fallen and looked for Bob.

"Oh, dear God, please, let him still be alive!"

But there was no chance of that. At the end of a long smear of blood, Bob's twisted body lay in the middle of the street.

Mike was weeping even before he'd run out to the corpse. Bob's head was cracked open like a walnut and a white mass of brains lay around it in a spreading puddle of blood.

Mike stared and wept like a baby.

CHAPTER 23

"Ms. Santos—the old lady who was walking her dog—says that the hit-and-run driver wore a ski-mask," Detective Shania Banks told Mike the next day when she visited him at home. "So she had no idea if the driver was male or female."

Mike nodded through a headache. This time Detective Banks looked like she'd gotten even less rest than the last time he'd seen her; her red hair was untidy and she had bags under her green eyes and seemed to have developed additional wrinkles on her forehead since he'd last spoken to her. Sitting on Mike's couch with her legs crossed and a notebook in hand, Shania Banks was the personification of the modern overworked woman.

"Ms. Santos also didn't take any note of the car's registration number," she went on. "But that doesn't really matter. We've already found the killer car."

"You have?" Mike asked, leaning forward in his chair, the armchair on her right.

After the police had taken their initial report about the incident and the Medical Examiner's office had taken away Bob's body, Mike had fallen into serious depression.

First of all he'd called Bob's parents and informed them of what had happened. Then he'd driven down to Taunton to see them and had accompanied them to the police station and morgue. Watching Bob's parents and sister Karen all break down in tears last night had been a truly miserable experience.

On returning back home, Mike had gotten a bottle of whiskey from the kitchen and had settled into some serious drinking. He'd drunk and wept for most of the night, only falling asleep in the wee hours of the dawn. His hangover now was the stuff classic novels were made of.

On waking up this morning, his first order of business had been to call in sick at work.

It had rained in the night and when Mike had walked out into the street after making that phone call, all the bloody signs of Bob's murder had been washed away. In a way the disappearance of the blood made things better; in another it made them worse.

With the minute portion of his mind that still cared, Mike wondered if his breath smelt really bad. If it did, Detective Banks' poker-face wasn't letting on. He admired her professionalism. But he still wished she'd hurry up and get through talking, so he could get back to drinking.

"Yeah, we found the damn car," Shania Banks said. "It had been abandoned across Broadway, over on the west half of Britton Street, near the B & D Construction Company . . . after which the killer apparently fled through the nearby woods. No fingerprints—the perp must've worn gloves . . ."

"Whose car was it?"

She scowled in disgust. "Some guy who was busy getting drunk in Rudy's Truck Stop at the time of the incident. The guy had already gotten a load on when he'd arrived at Rudy's, which is apparently how he forgot the car keys in the ignition. . . . Both Rudy and the waitresses swear he didn't leave the bar all evening. The girls are particular about this 'cos he'd been harassing them both to go back home with him. The one positive thing about this—if there's anything good about it— is that, on realizing the car was stolen, Bob Evans's death is now being investigated as a murder, and in line with that, we've also upgraded the investigation of Ashley Hunt's own death from a hit-and-run accident to a murder also."

Mike studied the detective's drawn face; suddenly he felt sympathy for her; for the crappy job she had to do; hunting down the scum of society so that they in turn couldn't hunt down the innocent. And then afterwards, after being strained and stained by all that, she still had to return to her family, to her husband and children and her dog, and somehow live a normal life like everyone else.

Still he wished she'd leave soon; his good buddy Jack Daniels was waiting to keep him company through the day. He was certain Jack must be feeling lonely by now.

"I can't help feeling that it was me the driver was really after," he said. "That makes it worse—that Bob died because of me. Shit! It was his birthday just last weekend and we had a great party . . . and . . ."

Shania Banks nodded sympathetically. "Mr. Evans's death forces us now to consider that possibility."

Mike's phone rang. He glanced at the screen.

"Hold on a minute, it's our friend Kirk," he told Detective Banks. "He's either just heard about Bob's death or wants to find out how my date with his hot cousins went."

Not feeling up to a verbal exchange over the phone at the moment, Mike tapped off a quick message telling Kirk that Bob was dead.

Kirk's response was immediate: 'What? Oh God no! How When?'

'Can't talk now, cops r here,' Mike tapped back. 'Speak to you later.'

'Okay, I'll come over to the house in a hour. SHIT! SHIT!'

That settled, Mike returned his attention to Detective Banks, who had waited patiently in the interim.

"But it's obvious, isn't it?" he said to her. "I mean, obvious that I'm the one the hit-and-run driver was really after yesterday. Hey, I know you don't believe me, ma'am, but now I'm back to thinking that even those murders at Master Slim's place are somehow connected to me."

"No, they're not," Detective Banks said with finality and with a grim and yet sympathetic smile on her face. "Mr. Broadman, those were gang-related killings. You need to try and accept that. Those were gangland deaths. Gory shit like that happens everyday. It's par for the course with hoodlums. Let it go." She sighed. "And to be honest, sir, I really don't think anyone is trying to murder you." She saw his skeptical expression and explained: "Yes, there have been two hit-and-run deaths of people associated with you, but . . . well, they really could be coincidental. You guys . . . and Ms. Hunt too, could merely have been the victims of a sicko who's twice stolen a car at random and driven around in it looking for someone to run down."

"Yeah sure, detective, whatever you say. I'll try not to act too paranoid."

Shania Banks sounded like she doubted her own explanation; she looked like she was amazed at the bullshit she was spouting. That was good enough for Mike. From this moment onward he was watching his back at all times.

The detective clearly discerned his thoughts, because she sighed. "All I'm saying, Mr. Broadman, is, don't jump to conclusions without any hard evidence."

Mike nodded dully. "Yah, O.K."

She asked him a few questions, took down a few notes and left.

Once she was gone, Mike filled a glass with whiskey, streamed the most depressing music he could find from his cellphone, and settled down to ignore the day.

This wasn't the same kind of drinking he'd done after Linda Dunning's death. Though intense and much greater than usual, his alcohol intake then had yet been regulated by his realization that he had to go to work in the morning. Indeed, he'd only drunk when he'd gotten in from work, and at the back of his mind there had lurked the consciousness that he mustn't overdo it. But now, he was trapped in a situation of even greater emotional pain, at a time where he had two whole days of nothing to do except grieve, and he felt he needed as much hard liquor as he could fit into these forty-eight hours, and as such was on a quest to fill up his soul with liquid mind-numbing inebriation.

***

Sometime in the afternoon, Kirk and Eddie stopped by. On their arrival the two brothers looked like they'd looked death in the face—that was how stunned they were by the bad news.

Everyone knew Bob as a bundle of life and energy, and to imagine he'd died so suddenly, and in such an arbitrary and violent way, was simply shocking. Mike told them the details of the killing—the murder—in a frigid voice that might have belonged to their dead friend's ghost.

He hadn't had the heart to post about Bob's death on social media for their circle of friends, so Kirk and Eddie did it for him.

The news of Bob's death had already spread along their street however and several of the neighbors (a number of whom had attended Bob's birthday party the previous weekend) came over to commiserate with Mike. Everyone was as depressed as hell and nobody said too much except to say how sorry they were that this had happened to Bob of all people.

Then, after a shopping trip to the stores by Kirk and Eddie to load up on booze, everyone did their damnest best to get as drunk as they possibly could.

Mike made sure he stayed well ahead of the others in the drunken marathon.

However, before he got too drunk to care, he did notice one oddity: Kirk kept grabbing hold of his crotch as if he had a really bad itch down there. He was doing his best to hide his discomfort, but it was glaringly obvious to Mike, who'd shared a house with him for over a year, and had known him for much longer. Mike supposed that Kirk had contracted VD from one of his many flings.

CHAPTER 24

Mike stopped drinking late on Saturday night because he ran out of booze. And by the time he ran out of booze, he was too drunk to find his way to his own front door, talk less of driving to the nearby liquor store to purchase some more whiskey.

Long story short, he passed out on his living room floor and didn't wake up till Sunday morning, by which time he'd peed all over himself, both had the world's worst hangover ever and felt completely sick, and also felt like he was dying of hunger to boot. He realized then that he'd not eaten a thing all through yesterday.

He woke up alone. Kirk, Eddie and their other friends had all left by about 9 p.m. last night.

After staggering to the toilet and throwing up, then staggering into the kitchen and pouring some orange juice down his throat, Mike felt slightly more like a human being and less like what a cat had passed out of its anus. He turned on the coffee maker, loaded some bread into the toaster and then staggered out of the kitchen to look for some aspirin. His head felt broken, like it would crack open if he didn't grip it firmly. Two successive mornings of Grade A-plus hangovers had him feeling half dead.

And all the while, as he performed the routines of the morning to put himself back in reasonable working order, the memories of why he'd been drinking so hard lurked in the back of his mind; a ghost that had no intention of being exorcized soon.

Bob! Dammit, Bob's dead!

It was hard to accept. From now on there would be no more of his smiling, joking bestie. No more 'dude, this' and 'dude, that'; no more carefree laughter, no more humor-tinged good advice.

When he died, he was laughing, joking about how the Lawrence sisters would be great for me!

Mike shut his eyes and for a moment he once again saw the vehicle that had snuffed out his friend's life—a mindless chunk of metal driven with evil intent, deadly and unstoppable . . .

Mike felt poised on the ledge of despair. Before him yawned an abyss; all he had to do was take a few steps forward and he could sink completely into the quicksand of his misery and vanish. Or in the alternative, he could continue to get drunk. Beer, wine, whiskey would tranquilize him, would lift him well above the emotional turmoil of the days to come. All he had to do was drive out to a nearby supermarket or liquor store and buy more alcohol.

But then he reconsidered: *The person who murdered Bob was actually trying to kill ME!*

Even though, as Detective Banks had pointed out, Mike had no clear-cut proof of this, it was nonetheless this thought that sobered him up, the chilling realization that until the police caught that hit-and-run killer, he was still in grave danger.

A drinking binge wouldn't help here, and neither would spacing out on his sorrow. He needed his senses both as sharp as knives and focused on his environment rather than on his pain.

So Mike cleaned himself up, had some breakfast, and then sat down to figure out what happened next in his life, if he had any say in it at all.

Still, most of the day seemed to go to waste. He felt lethargic. Sure, life went on after a bestie's death; but the hours dragged and sucked.

Mike was forced to accept that there was no chance of his feeling happy today. He considered calling up Kirk and Eddie and going to hang out with them; but knowing Kirk, that would wind up with the three of them getting drunk again to wash away their sorrows, and Mike intended to avoid alcohol for now, until he was certain he could drink it in moderation again.

That settled in his mind, he got out his laptop. Maybe doing some work would make the hours run faster. He and Brooke Lee still hadn't settled on where to install the speakers in the gym basement.

But after staring at the laptop screen for half an hour with the lines of the building's floor plans seeming to melt into blood before him, Mike quit on that too.

The impressions of blood slowly shifted his thoughts to dead Ashley Cummins, and from there to the equally dead Ashley Hunt and from there to the still-living Ashley Richard, aka Mortika.

Mortika the witch, the Ashley who got away.

So, yes, maybe it would be humiliating to ask his sort-of ex for help, but Mike sudden felt a desperate need to speak to her. He really needed to talk to someone who would understand his concerns about supernatural involvement in all these deaths occurring around him.

He called Mortika, but she didn't pick up. He left her voicemails. He sent her several text messages, but she didn't reply any of them. He considered driving over to her house to see if she was home, but then decided against it. If she was feeling bitchy, she'd call it stalking. She was obviously cooling him off; she most likely thought he wanted to get back together with her.

Hey, I could ask Kirk to talk to her for me. But . . .

But, Kirk was a total skeptic where supernatural things were concerned. He'd have better luck asking Eddie to talk to Mortika. Or, better yet, he could simply drop by her shop tomorrow. That was a place of business.

Bitchiness aside, she'll be more inclined to speak to me there. Particularly once I offer to pay her for both her time and advice.

He packed away his laptop again, turned on the TV and watched any number of sports shows. It didn't matter which ones they were—basketball, wrestling, baseball, soccer, hockey, golf, tennis. What counted was how the seemingly life-or-death concentration on the millionaire athletes' faces as they exerted their will to win entranced him for several hours. Morning slowly became noon and then late afternoon.

It was then, with the tension in his mind stretching to breaking point, that he reached the decision to drive out to Master Slim's place.

CHAPTER 25

The old house sat there exactly how he remembered it, a well-preserved relic from bygone days. The cops looked to have finished their investigations in the place because the yellow 'Crime Scene' tape had all been removed.

The two cars he'd noticed there on the day he'd found the bodies were still parked outside the building, but as he pulled up beside the vehicles a glance at them informed him that neither of them had been used since that day. Both vehicles had bird poop and twigs on their windshields and were covered with dust across which ran rain-trails.

If the house's surrounding grounds had previously seemed uncared for, now that the owners were dead that neglect had an additional sense of desolation to it.

As Mike alighted from his pickup truck, he appreciated the homestead's feeling of abandonment. He felt just the same as the place seemed to.

Yeah, house, the old guy's gone, huh? Don't take it too badly, Bob's gone too. But we'll both get over it with time and new friends.

Mike accepted the fact that he had no logical reason to come there. But just being here at the dead occultist's residence brought him a sort of solace. He couldn't explain it as other than the feeling that he and the house were perhaps comforting each other, and so he walked over to the place, climbed up to the front porch and sat there on the edge of the steps. Sitting there on that front stoop, he did some more thinking.

At the moment, nearby forest notwithstanding, this place both looked and felt more desolate than being out in the desert. Driving up the street past the three or four other driveways that led to houses, he'd not seen a soul. Maybe because it was Sunday; maybe because no one else really lived out here.

After a while of sitting on the porch and communing with the homestead's loneliness, Mike reached a decision. He got up, made his way back to his pickup truck, and rummaged around in the truck bed until he found a tire iron.

Armed with the tire iron, and with a grim look on his face, he made his way back to the old house.

***

Mike made no attempt to jimmy open the front door. He did test the doorknob to see if maybe the police had been careless and forgotten to lock it, but that wasn't the case, so he left the front door and walked around the house to its back door.

There has to be something inside here that can help me out! he told himself.

His plan was to search Master Slim's house until he found that 'something.'

He reached the back door, stuck the tire iron between the door and door jamb and gave the tire iron an almighty wrench. The door wood must have been very old, because with very little resistance, the portion of the door that housed the lock instantly splintered. Mike repositioned the tire iron and wrenched on it again. The door popped open, and the lock, along with the portion of wood that had held it in place, fell out of the door.

Mike scowled at the damage. *I'm gonna need to find a way to wedge it shut before leaving the house.*

Opening the door had made quite a bit of noise. Though he knew none would be forthcoming, Mike nervously listened for any sounds of investigation.

Then, once that concern had passed, he realized that he had an even graver matter to attend to. He left the tire iron on the floor inside the back door and hurried back around the house to his pickup truck.

Oops, I almost forgot that there's only supposed to be two vehicles parked out front. If any of the neighbors drives up this way and sees my pickup truck . . . they'll likely assume it's the drug dealers come back to ransack the place, and they'll call the cops!

Alarmed by this oversight, Mike drove his truck round to the back of the house, where it couldn't be seen from the road.

Then, after parking it, he returned to the back door of Master Slim's house and now entered the building.

The house interior gave off a similar vibe of absolute desolation to the surrounding land. Mike was struck by the impression of many ancient spirits having departed this place, fleeing like quail scattered by buckshot. Not just the old man's and his son's ghosts, but possibly the devils Master Slim had once summoned and communed with.

It was a chilling, extremely eerie feeling, and under normal circumstances, Mike would not have remained in this house for another minute.

But he felt desperate now, and so he would not let his fears dissuade him from his objective. After checking his watch and noting that the time was now 6 p.m., he hurried down the rear hallway towards the living room.

6 p.m. meant another two hours of daylight; hopefully more than enough time to search through the building. One thing he didn't want to do was to turn on the house lights at night or use a torch to finish up his search. Either of those options would be a dead giveaway that someone was lurking in the house.

Mike headed to the living room to search the bookshelves there. He needed literature about hexes, magic spells, whatever. Sure you could find just about anything on the internet nowadays, but this time he wanted it from the horse's mouth, not from Wiki, Reddit or Quora.

However, reaching the living room meant that Mike first had to traverse the room with the old man's hi-fi system and occult CDs, the room where he'd found the three severed heads. He gulped when he stepped in there and recognized that that was where he was. The blood pentagram was still drawn on the floor, along with a red blob in its middle that marked where the heads had been placed.

"And Detective Banks thinks drug dealers did this?" Mike queried aloud. "I'm never gonna look at cocaine the same way again."

He hurried from there into the parlor.

The living room was dark, with the drapes all drawn. After debating on the dangers of doing so, Mike parted the side drapes and flooded the room with light. The living room was still a mess, with wide swathes of blood on its walls and floor and furniture. Mike cringed at the gruesome reminders of those violently partitioned bodies he'd found. And the memory now brought him another worry:

But what if she's right and it really was drug dealers who killed everyone, and they come back to look for their drugs while I'm here? They're going to think that that's why I'm here too!

With scary images of his own chopped up body in his mind, Mike hurried across to the old man's bookcase. Working from top to bottom, he began reading the books' spines:

"Necromancy Made Simple . . . Necromancy Explained . . . Black Magic for White Witches . . . Encyclopedia of Occult Practices . . . Voodoo in New Orleans: 1849–1994 . . . Curses: Their Casting and Cures . . ."

Mike read the titles and felt stumped. He opened several of the books and gave up on noticing that a good amount of their text wasn't in English.

Where do I start from?

It occurred to him that it might be safer to just pack Master Slim's entire occult library outside into his pickup truck and take the books home, where he could study them at his leisure and without the threat of being caught doing so. But that approach, if it backfired, was certain to *really* get him in trouble with the law.

If I'm caught then it won't just be breaking and entering I'll be charged with, but burglary. And then it'll be farewell job, welcome jail cell.

So he kept searching through Master Slim's collection of occult literature, and the longer he looked, the more discouraged he became.

Down on the bookcase's fourth shelf, however, Mike found one book that stood out from the others. It was a small leather-bound book—about the size of a comic book.

'Necromantica Vol. 625: Summoning the Dead.'

Mike liked the fact that the book was thin—not much to read through—and was written entirely in English. He hated the fact that the leather this book was bound in had both the look and texture of human skin.

But still, he carried it over to the window so he could make out the text clearly and began reading through it.

It had suddenly occurred to Mike Broadman that he just might have the means here of summoning Ashley Cummins's ghost back from her grave again.

Yes, it was a scary action to consider, but one that seemed worth a try.

CHAPTER 26

Because the ritual to invoke the spirits of the dead required a pentagram to be drawn in blood on the floor, Mike opted to use the inner room where he had a ready-made bloody pentagram; he wasn't about shedding more of his blood than he needed to. Though the wound from Master Slim's puncturing of his forearm had since healed, its scar was a reminder and a warning of the pain to come.

Mike carried the square table near the bookcase into the inner room. Then he searched for the cup designed like a human skull into which Master Slim had collected his blood. He found the cup in a closet in the inner room along with the black ritual dagger that the old man had bled his arm with. Beside the cup and knife lay a box of black and red candles. He took the five black candles the spellbook explained he would need and then looked around for a lighter.

It was almost dark by the time Mike had gotten everything set up the way the spellbook instructed. But he no longer worried about being discovered; a sense of urgency fuelled his actions now, as if he was poised on the edge of a world-shaking discovery of his own.

On to the ritual then.

First, Mike returned to the living room and shut all the drapes again. And then, when once more standing in semidarkness, he lit the black candles that he had arranged at the five points of the blood-pentagram. The candles flickered up, filling the inner room with creepy half-light.

Spread open to the relevant pages, the skin-bound spellbook lay on top of the square table, with the skull cup and dagger lying beside it. Mike now picked both of the latter up.

He realized that he hadn't really paid much attention to the cup the last time he'd been here. The skull cup was a very gruesome-looking thing. Its design gave a very convincing impression of a soul in terrifying torments or at its moment of agonizing death. For a moment Mike almost dropped it—he'd had the sickening impression that it was the actual skull of someone who'd been abducted and beheaded. But then reason prevailed: the cup was made from wood, not bone.

It got darker outside. After gritting his teeth, Mike gashed the base of his left palm with the black ceremonial dagger.

He watched the blood well up in the wound and drip into the cup. He let it flow until it clotted, by which time the cup was about a quarter full. Then, ignoring the pain from the wound, he set the cup and knife back down on the table, picked up the opened spellbook and began reading:

"Nosrep da edu oy l'lacu oy l'laci!
Emot kaeps d na y lira rop met efil ot n'ruter,
Emot kaeps emoc sey!"

After reciting the spell, Mike suddenly felt lightheaded and the room felt like it was spinning around him.

No, I haven't lost enough blood to make me feel faint, he realized. *I think the spell is working.*

He staggered away from the pentagram and sat in one of the chairs by the door to the living room. He waited for the room to normalize again, but it didn't. Instead everything grew darker and then the bloody pentagram on the floor exploded into flames. The five candles around it instantly melted down to puddles of black wax. The pentagram flamed higher.

And suddenly there was something in the middle of the flames, but it was blurred and unclear. An incoherent visual representation. A suggestion of a shape that hinted of things to come. He was not disappointed by this; he had performed a different summoning ritual from Master Slim's and knew that a different procedure was certain, or at least very likely, to produce a different effect.

"Give me blood to grant me form, or else let me return to the torments of the Abyss," the shape said.

Mike recognized Ashley Cummins's voice.

"Hurry," she said. "Hurry, before I fade away from you."

Mike quickly got up, picked up the cup of blood and held it out to the blurred shape, which in turn extended equally blurred appendages to receive it from him.

She raised the cup to her indistinct head and after a slight pause he heard lip-smacking sounds indicating satisfaction.

He waited while the blurred form became a dead young woman. From being just a faint suggestion of colored lines in midair in front of him, suddenly she looked like a faded watercolor. And while he watched she grew more vivid and solid looking, like a pencil drawing being inked, like an oil painting acquiring human life.

Finally Ashley Cummins smiled at him from within the burning pentagram. "Hello, Mike, it's nice to see you again."

Mike now became aware that except for the blazing pentagram on the floor and the corpse standing inside it, the room had completely faded into shadows; it had no walls and the darkness beyond them both seemed to extend to infinity. Simultaneously he also realized that his heart was pounding and that now there was an intense terror thrumming inside him like a cascade of harp arpeggios.

He was also visually reminded that he'd not performed the same ritual Master Slim had. Last time Ashley had appeared fully formed; now she seemed to be struggling to exist here.

Ashley looked no better than she had the last time she'd appeared. She was still naked and her belly still looked like a botched cesarean section in which she'd given birth to her own intestines. The wound gaped bloodily in the middle of her torso, blood painted her legs crimson, and her intestines still hung down to her knees.

"Hello, Ash," Mike said. He'd have preferred not to look at her, but was worried that looking away might annoy her. And he wanted to ask her a few things.

The ghost finished drinking his blood and handed back the cup. Mike put the cup down on the table again.

Ashley frowned now. "Why have you summoned me? Get right to the point; we don't have much time to talk."

"Bob's dead."

"He is? That wasn't my doing."

"Are you sure of that? I mean as in, one hundred percent certain you had nothing to do with his death?"

Ashley regarded him with surprise. "How do you mean? I didn't kill Bob."

Despite the funereal off-white pallor of her skin and her mutilated belly, her facial expression looked so normal that Mike lost most of his fear of her. The undercurrent of potential terror still ran through him like an underground brook that intended to break through his surface, but he felt more properly in control of himself now. He already knew the score here: Ashley couldn't harm him except she left the pentagram, and she couldn't do that except he invited her outside of it, which he wasn't dumb enough to do.

I just have to keep her from losing her temper. I also have to ensure we don't get into any posthumous romantic discourses about my guilt over her suicide. She seems not to be thinking in that direction yet and I had better ensure I don't steer our conversation in any emotional directions.

While doing his best to avoid looking at her ghastly injury, Mike couldn't help thinking that this entire mess could have been avoided if Ash had simply liked Eddie Coombs as much as he liked her.

Mike stepped up closer to the flames. They weren't as hot as normal fire, but he wasn't taking any chance on burning his clothes, so he still kept a safe distance.

"Hey, I'm not saying *you* killed him, but . . . after the last time when Master Slim summoned you—"

"Mike, where is the old warlock? This ritual you summoned me with is much less potent than the previous one."

"Master Slim is dead, Ash."

Her expressionless eyes spread wide. "He is?"

"Yeah, that's why I'm doing this now instead of him. Someone killed him . . . and his son and his son's friend. Are you saying you aren't responsible for those deaths too?"

She looked bothered now. "Mike, why would *I* kill *him* . . kill *them*? What would be my motive for killing the warlock and his family?"

Mike stopped himself from angrily replying: "Because their surname was Brooks!" *Her response makes sense. She really has no motive to terminate their lives; or Bob's life either.*

"Do you know *who* killed them?" he asked her.

"No, I don't." The dead girl sighed and her voice was a miserable river; her pale throat a spring of eternal sadness. "Mike, once you're dead, you know a little bit more about how things work, but not that much. We spirits aren't omniscient—that's strictly God's territory. Even the Devil's knowledge is limited; most times he only finds out what's happened afterwards. And that goes for the good angels too." She smiled coldly. "For the human dead, we only know what we discover ourselves or are told of by others of our kind."

Mike nodded. "Fair enough. Now, here's the thing: Like I said, I'm not blaming you for killing those people, but . . ."

"But what, Mike? Speak quickly; we're running out of time."

She wasn't exaggerating. Her form was blurring, her vivid colors once again fading as if being bleached from her. The flames around her also seemed to be dying out, their height was lowering by the second.

"Can spells backfire?" he asked quickly. "That's my question. Sure, one sees it in movies all the time: dumb characters fuck up an incantation or something like that and the demons kill them all. . . . But . . . can a *properly cast* spell, one that's done right, go wrong?"

"No they can't, so long as you keep to the terms and conditions attached to the spell. And in this case those are simple—stay away from pussy that isn't attached to either a Brooke or an Ashley." Now she smiled coldly again. "Have you been keeping to those conditions, Mike? I'm asking because even though I haven't been following you about, my curse has . . ."

"Yes, I have," Mike said. "I'm strictly committed to dating Brookes and Ashleys now. Though I wish you'd just forgive and forget and let me live a normal dating life."

"That isn't ever going to happen. You made my bed and you're going to lie in it too. It isn't like I'm happy being dead either. So we're both paying the price in our different ways."

She was fading fast now, cosmic fabric being unraveled into its constituent threads, degenerating into a mere smudge on the window of mental perception. Mike felt relief as her dangling guts blurred into nonexistence.

But then, just before she became completely intangible again, a mere jumble of dangling spider webs amidst the fire, Ashley grinned: "Hey, Mike, there's something I do know for certain, and I'll share it with you if you like."

"Yes? What's that?"

"Those two conjoined girls? The Siamese twins?"

His eyes widened in surprise. "Brooke and Ashley Lawrence? Yeah, what about them?"

She laughed loudly and mockingly. "Those two girls are both madly head-over-heels in love with you. Goodnight, Mike, and thank you for the blood."

Still laughing, Ashley Cummins faded away to nothingness.

The flames died out and the room came back into being around him.

Mike stood there for a while, pondering on what she had told him and all the while being aware that something in the place was different. Some minor detail about the room had clearly altered, but what was it?

Oh, so the twins love me, huh? Oh, hell no! . . . Wow!

It had just hit him what the difference in the inner room was: the bloody pentagram on the floor was gone.

***

Mike got out of there in a hurry after that, but first he made sure to return everything to where he'd taken them from.

Before leaving he also got out his cellphone and took several snaps of the relevant pages of the skin-bound tome he'd cast the spell from.

There was no telling if and when he'd need to summon Ashley Cummins again.

He figured he could easily buy the rest of the items—Mortika had lots of skulls and chalices and ritual candles and ceremonial daggers in her shop, and he had sufficient blood left in his body for several more summoning attempts—but the summoning spell couldn't be duplicated.

He considered simply taking the spellbook along with him; but there was the off-chance that it might be missed by someone.

Outside, it was dark now. Mike wedged the back door of the house as tightly shut as he could with some ancient newsprint and then drove off.

He made certain to leave the truck lights off until he was back on the highway and heading safely for home.

The base of his left palm hurt where he'd gashed it, but he figured the trade-off had been more than worth it.

CHAPTER 27

"I can't believe Bob is dead," Brooke Lee told Mike when he arrived at the 3M gym on Monday morning to continue overseeing the installation of their new audio system. "I couldn't believe it when I saw the update on my friend Terri's WhatsApp profile and even now it's still like a bad dream."

Mike nodded. "The police are treating his death as a murder. They think he was run down by the same guy who killed another friend of ours."

This was of course news to Brooke. "They think you're being targeted by a serial killer?" she asked worriedly. "You're on his hit list too?"

Mike shrugged. "I dunno." He was relieved, however, that she'd not enquired about the identity of the dead friend. He was starting to really like her and he didn't want her thinking she'd be in danger if she associated too closely with him. "I was walking with Bob at the time and the car didn't seem to be making any distinctions between us. I'm lucky to still be alive. Otherwise we'd both be in the funeral home now."

Brooke looked even more shocked. "For real?"

"For real, girl."

Mike stroked the large Band-Aid at the base of his left palm. He felt much more composed today. Strange as it had turned out to be, yesterday's trip to Master Slim's place had been catharsis to his troubled soul. Yes, Bob Evans was dead, but life went on. So sad and yet so true.

The process of summoning and speaking to Ashley Cummins's ghost had been both troubling and soothing, but with emphasis on the latter.

However, Ashley could keep the Siamese Lawrence twins and their supposed head-over-heels devotion to him. Mike wanted a 'normal' woman.

He and Brooke Lee were up on the second floor, in the building's secondary cardio room, and Mike glanced away from her for a moment, his vision trailing around the room, flitting from one piece of exercise equipment to another. Over in a corner, a technician was servicing a treadmill; in another area the Cashstretch crew were hoisting a large loudspeaker up to its perch at the top of a support pillar. As Brooke had explained it to him, lots of the gym's clients brought their own sounds to listen to on their earphones, and as such the loudspeakers wouldn't really be as useful up here as in the resistance machines rooms on the ground floor, for instance, or the pool or sauna, but the new owners wanted to have the potential to adjust the functions of each of the gym's rooms on a moment's notice. Which meant everywhere had to have the same audio capabilities. Mike had proposed a matrix-amplifier setup, where each room could be fed a different mix of audio signals depending on its required function.

Mike nodded to the guys installing the speakers and returned his attention to Brooke.

"When is the funeral?" she had just asked him.

"Wednesday afternoon. He's being cremated. It's a closed casket affair 'cos his head is totally destroyed and there's no way that the undertakers can ever make it look presentable."

"Ugh, that's just awful," Brooke said. "Where's the funeral being held? I'd like to attend the service."

"The Sowiecki Funeral Home in Taunton. Hey, why don't we just go together? I've gotten the afternoon off to attend, so I can just drive down here and pick you up."

"Yeah, that'll be cool," Brooke agreed.

Mike's phone rang then. It was Detective Shania Banks. "It's the cops," he told Brooke, then accepted the call.

"Good morning, detective, how are things?"

"Mr. Broadman, what the hell is the matter with you?"

"Huh?" Brooke looked surprised at the surprise on his face. "What are you talking about? I haven't done anything."

Shania Bank's voice was cold; he was immediately reminded of those frigid green eyes of hers like slimy jail cells. "I'm talking about you going over to the old man's house yesterday and messing about in there."

Mike felt chilled. "Er . . . how'd you know about that?"

"We're the police, Mr. Broadman! Knowing things like that is our job."

"You've been following me? Am I a suspect too?"

He heard her sigh; a loud exhalation of exasperation. "No, no, you idiot, we're not goddamned following you—we've real criminals to chase. We rigged up the Brooks' house with security cameras in case those damned drug dealers came back to look for their merchandise. And who do we catch on candid camera this morning when we review the footage?"

"Me," Mike said dully. Brooke Lee had just been on a phone call of her own. Now she gestured to him that she had to get downstairs and he nodded.

"Yes, you!" Detective Banks agreed. "Mr. Broadman, I thought we already agreed that Master Slim was murdered by drug dealers? So what the hell were you doing trying out witchcraft in there, huh?"

"I-I-I . . . Uh?" Mike really had no explanation for that.

"You're lucky you didn't burn the place down with that fire you started in the inner room. I'm in half of a mind to book you right now for breaking into the place and messing with a police investigation as well as tampering with evidence . . . but—"

"What else did you catch on tape?" Mike interrupted.

"What are you talking about? And I wasn't done speaking yet."

"Yeah, yeah, I know. What I mean is, after I lit the candles, what else did the cameras catch?"

"Nothing, literally nothing. You lit the candles, cut your hand and began muttering all that mumbo jumbo and then the floor caught fire and then everything went blank as a black wall. The cameras didn't record anything else until you're back replacing everything to where you'd taken them from. Why do you want to know?"

Mike wasn't about telling her the real reason. The cameras hadn't filmed Ashley's presence in the building then. So Detective Banks would continue to disbelieve any kind of a supernatural explanation he might give her.

"Nothing really," he replied. "I just wanted to know if maybe something happened in there."

"What kind of 'something' were you expecting to happen, sir?" He could literally *hear* her patience with him wearing gossamer thin over the phone connection. *At the moment I'm this close to landing myself in a jail cell. How in the world didn't I consider the possibility that the cops might have wired Master Slim's place for sound and vision?*

"I'm feeling really desperate after Bob's death and I was wondering if maybe I could summon up his ghost," he replied the angry policewoman.

"You need a psychiatrist then, sir, not a medium. Grief over the loss of a close friend or loved one is a normal, natural process . . . and there's no such things as damn ghosts!" For a while she breathed heavily over the line, while Mike glanced over at the technicians installing the loudspeakers and gave them a thumbs-up. Then she said: "Now, listen up—this is the only warning you'll get from me. You ever pull a stunt like that again and I will book you. Do you understand me?"

"Yeah, sure, ma'am."

"Do you understand me, Mr. Broadman? You pull one more stunt like this and you'll be on trial for stupidity."

"Yeah, yeah, I hear you loud and clear. Ma'am, I'm sorry I broke the law yesterday and thanks for giving me a break now. I do appreciate it. Hey, any developments in your investigations into the hit-and-runs?"

"Nothing but exhaust fumes. Yeah, one more thing: you're paying for that busted back door."

Mike nodded at the opposite wall. "Yeah, sure, will do."

"Okay, goodbye, and have a nice day. I gotta get back to working the case. Don't worry—the murderer is gonna be caught sooner than he thinks."

"Have a nice day too, detective."

Shania Banks hung up.

Realizing he'd gotten off with barely a slap on the wrist, Mike hurried downstairs to find Brooke Lee again and ask her to have lunch with him at the McDonald's down the road.

He felt relieved that Brooke had had to leave the room during his phone call; it wouldn't do to have to explain to her exactly what he'd been up to yesterday. She'd think he was kooky.

As he descended the stairs to the ground floor Mike thought up a quick and logical explanation for the earlier portion of the phone conversation that she had overheard.

***

Okay, so normally Mike wouldn't have left Cashstretch at lunchtime, but he wasn't in the office today, so . . .

He parked the Ford pickup truck in the McDonald's parking lot, but then, before he and Brooke alighted from the vehicle, he looked across the road, over at Mortika's 'Jewelry, Fortunes and Spells' shop. There was a 'Closed' sign in the shop window.

That was very disappointing; he'd been hoping he could pop over there after work.

But then he noticed Eddie Coombs walking along the opposite sidewalk. Eddie was headed in their direction and was carrying a pair of shopping bags.

"Hold on a minute, I'll be right back," Mike told Brooke.

He got down from the truck, waited for a lull in the traffic and then dashed across the highway, calling out, "Eddie, Eddie!"

Eddie noticed him and waved. They met up on the sidewalk with Mortika's shop in the background.

"Hi, Mikey, what's up today?" Eddie greeted in his usual lackluster way. "Me, I'm just doing some shopping, man." Then he pointed across the road. "Who's the new girlfriend?"

Mike laughed. "Not a girlfriend yet, dude, but I'm workin' on it. At the moment she's still just a lady I know from work." He waved over at the truck, waiting until he'd caught Brooke's attention and she waved back at him.

"Yeah, cool to see that you're bouncing back." Eddie smiled for a few moments and then his expression turned sad. "Oh, man, but I still can't get over Bob's death."

Mike nodded. "I know exactly how you feel, man. It really sucks." Then he jerked a thumb at the 'Closed' sign on the Goth-themed storefront a short distance from them. "Hey, Eddie, have you seen Mortika lately? I haven't driven past here in a while . . . and yesterday I couldn't get her on the phone."

Eddie's normally placid expression now turned amused. "Man, I haven't seen her since she and Kirk parted ways . . . which happened right the next day."

Mike nodded. Yeah, one night stands were routine enough for Kirk. "But . . . Eddie, what's so funny?"

Eddie first looked around to see if anyone else was close by, and then, after confirming that no one would overhear him, he said: "Kirk's at the clinic. Mortika gave him an STD!"

Mike stared at him. "An STD? What the . . . ? She had the clap or crabs or . . . ? C'mon, dude, she wasn't HIV-positive, was she?"

Eddie looked pensive for a moment. "Ah, man, when you say 'dude' like that I just remember Bob all over again."

"Eddie, about the STD? What did kind of STD did Mortika give Kirk?"

Eddie shook his head like he was confused. "That's the thing, man. I don't know what it was. Never seen anything like it before, but Kirk's dick is like . . . The doctors still don't know what to make of it either!"

Mike just stared at him and nodded stupidly.

Eddie added: "Didn't you notice on Saturday when were at your place, how he kept on grabbing his dick like it was hurting him?"

"Yeah, I noticed that. I thought he had jock itch or something."

"Jock itch, my ass; the doctors say they've never seen anything like what Kirk's got!"

Eddie burst out laughing, and Mike let him laugh. Eddie's distraction was helping him conceal his own shock. *Mortika had an STD? Oh, so that's what Master Slim meant when he warned me against dating her? And according to what Eddie's just said, whatever it is must be particularly virulent. I don't envy Kirk one bit.*

Mike said a silent thanks to the late Master Slim and returned his attention to Eddie.

"It's kinda poetic, don't'cha think?" Eddie asked. "My bro is known for screwing everything in a skirt that's got a hole between its legs and . . . yeah, I do feel for the guy, but . . ."

He calmed down and gestured across the road at Mike's truck. "Say, won't your date be getting lonely?"

Mike shrugged. "Yeah, I guess I'd better be getting back to Brooke. But, Eddie, so where the hell is Mortika?"

Eddie shrugged too and shifted his bags from his left to his right hand. "No idea, man, and I don't wanna know either." He grimaced.

"That chick is crazy—you know? She's totally loco. When Kirk refused to date her she swore that she was gonna hex him."

Mike gaped at Eddie. "What? She claimed she was gonna *what?*"

Eddie nodded. "Yeah, you heard me right. Mortika said she was gonna put a magic spell on Kirk that would make him repulsive to women forever."

Eddie pointed first at the 'Jewelry, Fortunes and Spells' shop window and then tapped his head with his index finger. "Man, the pretty gothic lady has more than a few screws loose upstairs. And . . . and the way she looked when threatening Kirk like that scared me shitless. Me, I'm delighted to never have to see her again."

Mike was suddenly filled with an intense dread; the fear that Mortika was also dead, with her rotting corpse lying somewhere, unfound and untended. For a moment the idea filled him with vivid terror; and then he sighed in frustration.

It's crazy, but I can't even tell the police my fears. Detective Banks will simply shrug off my very rational and logical worries as more paranoia on my part.

But there was nothing he could do about it. Mortika had lived alone and even if she was actually missing, he didn't know any of her friends or her family; no one he could ask to file a missing persons report on her behalf.

***

"That guy you were talking to looks very familiar," Brooke remarked as she and Mike walked towards the McDonald's' entrance. "He was at Bob's party the other night, right?"

Mike nodded dully. "Yeah, that's Kirk Coombs's younger brother Eddie."

Brooke instantly pouted in disgust. "Oh, you mean Kirk the jerk?"

"Please don't tell me you've dated him too," Mike said. "Almost every girl I know has. They lust after him passionately until he dumps them and then afterwards they hate him just as passionately."

"Humph!" Brooke snorted in disgust. "I wouldn't let Kirk touch me in a million years. He's a total creep."

Mike smiled, remembering that Jane had also referred to Kirk as a creep before jumping into bed with him.

"Just for the record, you aren't a lesbian, are you?" he whispered as they joined one of the customer queues. Even though he'd lowered his voice, a few other lunchtimers looked over at them in amusement.

"You ask me that one more time and I'll break your arm," Brooke retorted. She clearly wasn't amused by the question.

"I'm not trying to insult you," Mike explained as the line moved forward. "It's just that the gay girls seem the only ones immune to Kirk's evil charms."

"No, I'm not a fucking dyke," Brooke whispered into his ear. "I'm straighter than your dick."

"Thanks, I'm very glad," Mike whispered back, while noting that his penis actually curved upward when erect. "Hey, will you break my arm too if I ask if you've got a boyfriend?"

She blushed then, which Mike took to mean she was available to be romanced.

"Hey," he asked, "would you really have broken my arm just now?"

She shook her head. "Not really, man. I do some MMA, but it's all for self-defense; I'm not looking to hurt anyone." She grinned. "You look surprised, but that's one reason why the gym's owners employed me—they want to include some basic MMA training at the gym."

Mike nodded in quiet satisfaction. *At least she'll prove much harder to kill than her predecessor.*

They were quiet while the McDonald's' servers filled their trays for them.

"Hey, you look really bothered," Brooke said as they walked over to the dining area. "Did Kirk's brother tell you some bad news?"

Mike shook his head and forced a smile, his mind on the possibly missing Mortika. "I'm just wondering if the driver who ran Bob down could have been a woman," he told Brooke.

CHAPTER 28

Two days later it seemed as if everyone in Raynham had put their own lives on hold and had gathered to pay their last respects to Bob Evans.

Taunton's Sowiecki Funeral Home was filled with people. Bob Evans's funeral was literally a repeat of his birthday party, but with everyone's happiness replaced by sadness.

Everyone wept. The general degree of sorrow was uniform. In a marked contrast to the normal state of affairs on such miserable occasions, it was impossible to differentiate Bob's family from his friends and employers merely by observing how grieved they were.

Rosemary Finch, the busty young woman who'd slept with Bob on the night of his birthday wept so much that Mike began suspecting that maybe Bob had gotten her pregnant like they'd both joked.

For Mike, being packed inside the funeral home with so many other unhappy people felt incredibly claustrophobic; not in a physical sense, as the building was quite spacious, but he felt as if the general atmosphere of shared misery was compressing him, feeding itself and growing larger while in turn making him smaller.

He glanced at Brooke Lee, who was seated on his left with her hands folded in her lap. She looked sad but not otherwise discomfited; nor did anyone else in the hall seemed troubled by more than their grief.

Mike decided that the unusual way he felt was due to his supernatural experiences of the past few days. At the moment, very little would surprise him, not even Bob's ghost suddenly appearing in front of him.

Having arrived late, he and Brooke were seated at the rear of the hall. He could make out Kirk and Eddie up front, seated almost directly behind Bob's parents and his younger sister. Rudy the truck stop owner was also seated behind the Evanses. Mike also thought he saw Detective Banks amongst the mourners, but he wasn't sure.

He felt intense relief when the funeral ceremony was over and he could step outside again.

***

After Brooke had offered her condolences to Bob's parents, Mike pulled her aside and together they walked off to stand beneath some trees. After a while Kirk and Eddie walked over to join them.

Mike hoped Kirk wouldn't start grabbing his crotch like the last time he'd seen him. But Kirk seemed to be okay now. He even seemed well enough to flirt.

"Hi, babe," Kirk said to Brooke, turning on the charm and flashing her his smoothest smile. "Been ages since I saw you last."

"It was just last Saturday," Brooke said flatly.

"Yeah well, whatever. For me, one day's the same as one year where a beautiful woman is concerned. What I mean by that is, it's always too long between meetings."

Despite herself, Brooke smiled at the compliment.

Mike began feeling worried. *Exactly what is this guy's problem?* he wondered about Kirk. He looked helplessly at Eddie. Eddie shrugged back, with a facial expression that said—*Hey, buddy, I already warned you not to leave your fresh milk where the cat can get to it.*

"Anyway," Kirk told Brooke, "I really think both of us should get together sometime and catch up . . . and maybe do a few other things too."

From the leer on Kirk's face when he said this, there could have been no doubt in Brooke's mind what he meant by 'other things.'

Mike shrugged in acknowledged defeat. *Looks like I just lost another girl . . .*

But, still grinning coyly, Brooke's reply to Kirk was: "Thanks for the offer, man, but I'm with Mike now."

"I can see that. I meant, let's hook up sometime when you *aren't* with him. Like later tonight, or over the weekend maybe if you prefer? Hit me up, honey, and let's set it up."

Brooke laughed. "Sorry if I didn't clarify either. What I meant was, at the moment I'm dating Mike, and I never double-date." To emphasize her point, she stepped closer to Mike and took his hand in hers.

Kirk rolled his eyes and looked exasperated. Mike hid his own confusion.

Eddie began laughing. "Hey, bro, I never thought I'd see this happen. You just had a woman turn you down publicly in Mikey's favor." He shrugged. "Maybe Mortika really did hex you and it's begun working."

"But maybe, Kirk," Brooke said with a deadly gleam in her eye, "maybe, if Mike doesn't want my pussy, I might give you a chance to kiss it. But don't get your hopes up, man."

Mike held his breath. Kirk looked mad now and his rage almost distorted his handsome face. But he controlled himself and managed a condescending smile at Brooke. "You don't know what you're missing, girlie."

"I know exactly what I'm missing and I wanna keep missing it."

Their stalemate might have continued, but then Eddie said, "Hey, Mikey, Brash are here too, you know. They were asking after you earlier."

"Who is Brash?" Brooke asked.

Mike shrugged. " 'Brash' are Kirk's twin cousins. He set me up on a date with them, but it didn't work out."

Brooke looked first at Kirk and then at Mike. "Why would he set you up with *two* girls?"

"Because Brash sort of do everything together?" Eddie said cryptically.

" 'Brash' is a weird name for a set of twins," Brooke said. "Don't they have individual names at all?"

Eddie shrugged. "They're a weird pair of young women."

"Hey, I gotta get a move on," Kirk interjected into the conversation with a broad gesture. "Wow, I look over there and see quite a few hot chicks in dire need of the TLC that Brooke here just turned down."

"Oh, they can have you," Brooke said. "Me, I'm very pleased with what I've got here." She was still holding onto Mike's hand, and now she leaned up and kissed him gently on the lips. Mike slipped his arm around her shoulders.

Kirk looked angry again and kicked a clump of grass. But then he smiled and smoothed down his suit. "C'mon, Eddie, don't hang around waiting for Mike's sloppy seconds."

"Yeah, yeah." Eddie trudged off after him.

Brooke frowned after them. "I totally can't stand Kirk. He acts as if once he smiles at you, you're obliged to sleep with him."

"Nah, you got me for that," Mike said.

Brooke smiled coolly up at him. "Not so fast, man; I like taking things slowly until I trust the guy."

Mike shrugged. "That's fine with me."

He felt fine. It was strange the way their relationship had suddenly metamorphosed from friends to . . . in the matter of a few minutes. *I've got Kirk to thank for that though. It's almost like she's hitched herself to me so she won't have to go to bed with him.*

"Hey, baby," Brooke said, "I need to go talk to a friend of mine over there. She pointed at a tall, plump woman over on their right who was about to get into a silver BMW convertible. "Hey, Maria!"

Mike watched her walk off. Black clothes, pale skin; entirely breathtaking.

The crowd of people in front of the funeral home had thinned now as the funeral attendees had begun dispersing. There would be a small funeral reception at the Evans's home, but most people here weren't expected to attend it. It was weird how Mike could almost feel the misery emanating from them all and evaporating into the atmosphere to form clouds of sadness, maybe to fall like rain at someone else's intense bereavement.

Then he sighted Bob's junior sister Karen standing slightly apart from the group of relatives and set off towards her. He wanted to tell Karen that he'd not be driving directly to her parent's house in Taunton after leaving here, but would first be taking Brooke home.

Karen was standing in direct line-of-sight to where Brooke was having an animated conversation with her friend. Mike thought he heard Brooke mention Kirk twice.

"Yeah, I guess Kirk really does get on her nerves," he muttered to himself, and then froze when a pair of hands grabbed him from behind.

"Take one more step away from our hearts and you're fucking dead, buster!" a familiar voice said.

"Yeah, now turn around real slowly, and keep your hands where we can see them, and your dick in your pants," another familiar voice said. Then both voices burst into loud giggles.

Mike sighed. The Lawrence twins had found him.

He turned around and managed to smile at them.

Best way that Mike could describe it, at the moment the twins looked like they worked for the FBI. Women in Black or whatever. They wore an extra-wide grey skirt suit (Mike was still having difficulty wrapping his mind around the tailoring or architectural prowess required to design clothes that fit these Siamese twins so immaculately) with a white silk blouse beneath it, dark sunglasses and sedate black handbags which nonetheless give the impression of containing weapons. Black tights and black shoes. Bright purple lipstick, which looked as striking as if someone had pasted an eggplant skin across their mouths. Their blonde hair was identically piled up behind their heads and secured with oriental-looking clasps.

Mike had to agree that the twins looked captivating. Yes, they looked admirably freaky. And that Secret Service vibe was unmistakable; Brooke and Ashley Lawrence looked as if they were 'on the case,' whatever the case was.

I just hope their case isn't me, Mike thought.

"Hi, ladies, you both look stunning today," he said. Which, annoyingly, was the truth.

They grinned back at him. "We've been looking all over for you."

"I got here late. Had some work I had to clear up first."

And then just like that, both twins' smiling expressions faded from their faces. "Oh, Mike, we're so, so sorry," Brooke said. "We didn't mean to treat you so badly the other night."

"Oh yes, really," Ashley said. "We're really, really sorry we behaved like that; it's just that sometimes the stress of being together all the time gets to us and we find it hard to control our anger about our condition and we wind up turning on each other."

"Please, Mike, please give us another chance."

"Yes, please do. We promise to make it worth your while."

"We'll be really good to you."

"And we'll be really good for you too."

Mike now remembered what Ashley Cummins's ghost had told him, that these two conjoined young women were both head-over-heels in love with him. To reassure himself that he wasn't about to once more fall under their spell of prettiness and date them again, Mike glanced behind them at Brooke Lee, who was still deep in conversation with her friend.

"Well, well . . . well . . ." he hedged, trying to choose his words with care, wondering how to let them know he now had a girlfriend without hurting their feelings and breaking their hearts. Because they both looked so earnest that he had the suspicion that one wrong word from him would break them both into tears.

"Oh, please, please, please, tell us that you've forgiven us and you'll go out with us again."

"Yes, Mike, please!"

Mike peered between their heads. Brooke's friend was driving off now, and Brooke was looking around for him. Seeing as he was taller than the twins, she'd soon notice him and head over this way, and once she did, he didn't want to imagine Brash's reaction to her.

"Okay," he said quickly. "I forgive you both. As of this moment, we're friends again."

"You do?" Ashley asked. "We are?"

"Oh, wow. That's really sweet of you, Mike."

"So you'll go out with us again?"

"Yes, when?"

Mike thought on it. This was the delicate part of the situation, and he had to handle it quickly. Brooke Lee was already walking over to he and the twins. This issue had to be resolved before she arrived here and he introduced her to them. Brooke's progress towards their trio was however being slightly delayed by her disbelief that the two young women she was approaching were joined together. At the moment she'd stopped in her tracks and was gaping at them.

"Okay, sure," Mike told the twins in a rushed and low voice. "I'll give you a call tomorrow and we'll set something up. How's that?"

Ashley pouted. "Why tomorrow? Why can't we go dancing at Rudy's tonight?"

"Yeah, Rudy is delighted with his website and he's promised to treat us the next time we're there."

Mike shook his head. "I can't. I've got a date for tonight. A business date," he quickly corrected on seeing the hurt look on their faces. "Just play along," he whispered desperately. "I promise to call both of you tomorrow."

Dammit! He had no idea what he was going to do tomorrow.

Brooke joined them. "You two girls must be 'Brash,' " she said immediately. "Hi, I'm Mike's girlfriend Brooke."

"Girlfriend?"

"Girlfriend?" The twins gaped at Mike.

"Listen," Mike said hurriedly, "why don't you three get properly acquainted? I've gotta talk to Bob's sister Karen before the family leaves here."

"Hey, Mike, come back here!" Brooke called out as he hurried off, leaving the three women alone.

"Yeah, come back here right now, Mike!" Ashley seconded. "We wanna talk to you!"

Mike kept going. "I'll call you both tomorrow like I promised!" he shouted back at the twins.

CHAPTER 29

"Those are some really weird young women," Brooke Lee said as Mike drove away from the funeral home.

"You don't know the half of it," Mike said. "You've honestly no idea what they're like."

"In or out of bed?"

He took his eyes of the road for a moment and frowned at her. "Out of bed. In bed, they're just like any other women: wanting, loving, passionate and vulnerable. But afterwards . . ."

"Hmmm. . . . Wanting, loving, passionate and vulnerable? With those stellar sexual qualities, are you sure you wouldn't rather be with them than with me?"

"Please stop teasing me. Those girls would drive me crazy if I lived with them for even twenty-four hours."

"Sometimes crazy is worth it. I know several emotionally unstable women who've got doting boyfriends and husbands who can't live without them and who don't even cheat on them. It just takes an accepting personality to live with someone like that."

"That's just sexism. You wouldn't take that stance if I was a woman and the emotionally-challenged party was a man. Then you'd be advising me to get the hell out of Dodge already."

"I'm just saying that emotional instability in a relationship might be compensated for by other factors."

Mike didn't understand what Brooke's problem was. She seemed to be testing him, to see how far she could push him. Or, was she perhaps hinting him of her own mental imbalance? He sighed. Why was the arena of male and female emotional combat always so indirect? Nothing was ever stated clearly and to the point, not even when it appeared to be. There were always subtle shades of meaning tacked onto the words, hints and threats that said, "Hey, I can't tell you exactly what I really want from you because I don't know it myself, but you had better be able to figure me out and give me exactly what I need, or else . . ."

The war between the sexes should be fought in bed! Mike thought with a sudden uncharacteristic surge of anger. *The war between the sexes should be fought in bed!*

Then he smiled at his lovely passenger and turned onto her street.

"Nice place you got here," he said as he pulled up in front of Brooke's bungalow. Earlier, he'd picked her up from work as agreed, and so this was his first time of being here. It was a small building, set back from the road at the end of a flower-lined driveway.

"Hey, why don't you come inside and let me fix you a sandwich?" Brooke said to him. "Considering that neither of us had any lunch, you've gotta be as hungry as I am."

Mike looked at his watch and then shook his head. "It's getting on to 4 p.m. I told Bob's sister Karen I'd join them at home as soon as I dropped you off."

Men have no immunity against women. Brooke flashed Mike a smile and he instantly felt like he was melting. "Oh, come on inside," she insisted nicely. "It'll only take a few minutes."

Mike nodded and killed the pickup's engine. "Yeah, well I really am hungry."

They got down together and walked up to the house.

***

"Wow, really nice place you got here," Mike said as he walked into Brooke's living room.

"You already said that outside," Brooke joked, slipping her arm through his.

"I really mean it. Best of all, it's very neat. It's not like my place, which is a mess all the time."

Brooke laughed. "I know. I saw it when I needed to use the bathroom during the party. *Men.*" She tugged on his arm. "Hey, come on into the kitchen with me while I prepare our food."

He followed her into her kitchen and leaned against the counter while she got bread and lunch meat and cheese and pickles out of the fridge.

She slid Mike a can of soda. "Hey, what are you gonna do about the twins?"

"Huh?" He popped the tab on the soda can and took a long gulp.

"Yes," Brooke said as she sliced bread, a serious expression on her face. "From the little I heard the twins say after you ran off and left us alone, they're seriously stuck on you. And I heard you tell them you'd call them tomorrow. What do you intend to do then?"

Mike sighed. "I'm going to let them know it won't work out between us, that's all. There's nothing else that I can do. They're nice . . . but . . . I owe it to myself and to you to make it crystal clear to them that there's no chance of us having any kind of a relationship."

Brooke finished adding slices of chicken to both sandwiches and then grinned. "They're gonna take it badly."

Mike shrugged. "I know. But what else can I do?"

"I dunno," Brooke admitted with an edge to her voice. "But do you recall what you were saying on Monday, about how the hit-and-run killer might be a woman?"

Mike looked at her narrowly and then shook his head and laughed. "Aw, come on now. You're not suggesting that the twins killed Bob, are you? I've heard of female jealousy, but even to go *there* is ludicrous."

Brooke shrugged. "I'm just saying you need to be careful with those two. They strike me as the stalking type who can't take no for an answer, and now that they're fixated on you, who knows what lengths they'll be prepared to go to, to eliminate the competition."

Mike suddenly got it: "You're thinking of yourself, aren't you? You're scared someone's gonna try and bump you off too."

She nodded and then quickly shook her head and struck a martial arts pose. "I'm a tough girl. I can look after myself. I just don't like having to look over my shoulder all the time."

Mike sighed. "Me neither. Hey, I'll try to make myself worth it."

Brooke grinned at him. "You'd better be worth it. I don't wanna wind up wishing I'd picked your jerk of a friend over you."

Mike shook his head. "Kirk and I? We're not really friends anymore. I just don't know how to get rid of the guy. Kirk's become— how can I put it? . . . Say, like old furniture that I can't throw out?"

"I've got a few friends like that myself," Brooke agreed. "I'd rather I didn't know them, but I've known them for so long that they've become a part of my life, like an old scar that still itches sometimes." She laughed. "But back to those conjoined exes or your—Brash. When you talk to them tomorrow, honey, please make it clear that if they dare come gunning for me, I'll break them both in two . . . right down the middle."

"They might like that; I think they're dying to be separated. Only there's no way it's gonna happen except maybe if one of them dies."

Brooke handed him a sandwich. "Hey, don't be so damn morbid. No one's killing anyone anymore. Let's eat."

CHAPTER 30

After Mike left her house, Brooke sat in her living room and did some thinking.

Okay, I think I handled things well today. Yes, I did.

Mike was right in one sense; she had latched onto him today primarily to get Kirk off of her back. During those moments when Kirk had been flirting with her she'd felt desperate enough to instantly elevate her platonic relationship with Mike to that of almost-lovers. But really, by doing so Brooke knew she had merely accelerated what would shortly happen—it was glaringly obvious to her that Mike wanted her as his girlfriend and would soon talk about them becoming a couple.

He's cute, she thought. *I just hope he treats me good.*

Her last boyfriend hadn't treated her well. They had broken up four months ago after she'd realized he was sleeping with two other girls as well as herself. Since then she'd avoided dating anyone. But then Mike had come along and she'd felt her frozen heart melting again.

What she liked most about Mike Broadman was his simplicity; he wasn't affected like most other guys she'd known. Sure, he was bold and confident, but he seemed satisfied to be who he really was—she liked men who kept it real. Mike was definitely nothing at all like Kirk.

Yes, Kirk is utterly gorgeous, but why does he have to be such a creep all the time?

Brooke wasn't looking for much in a man, just good looks and honesty. And true love of course. Where she was concerned, true love was the most important thing in a relationship.

She yawned. Being at home in the early evening during the week was unfamiliar to her and made her feel sleepy.

Then she looked up and sighed.

Oh, Mike forgot his cellphone.

She did some quick math in her head, calculating how long it had been since he left her house and comparing that to the time it would reasonably take him to drive down to Taunton and back here again.

She shrugged. He had to have arrived at Bob's parents' place by now. Which meant he wouldn't be returning here for a while.

She grinned to herself. *But oh, he definitely will be coming back here later. Or . . . or I could drive over there and hand him the phone. Bob's parents' address has to be on the WhatsApp funeral invite Kirk the jerk posted. Damn it, I'm too tired now tho'. Maybe later, after I've had a snort nap . . . if Mike still isn't back here by then, I'll drive down to Taunton to find him.*

She got up and walked into her bedroom and lay down in bed without getting undressed. In a few minutes, she was fast asleep.

***

A noise woke Brooke up. All of a sudden she was awake, alert and filled with a sense of danger.

She sat bolt upright in bed, with her breath coming fast and her pulse racing.

What is the matter? she wondered as she dropped her legs over the side of the bed and stood up.

I think someone is in the house. There's an intruder in my house.

Though alarmed, this knowledge did not particularly frighten Brooke Lee. She was too well-versed in the arts of self-defense to panic simply because her personal space had been breached. This was one of the first lessons she had learnt as a martial artist: never to panic when faced with a conflict situation, because panic lent itself to erratic thinking and erratic thinking made one make mistakes.

Hey, maybe it's Mike, come back for his cellphone. How long have I been sleeping for anyway?

The sky outside her bedroom windows was still clear and bright with no hint of dusk, so she couldn't have been asleep for too long.

But no, that couldn't be Mike out there. Even if she *had* left the front door open (and she was certain she hadn't), her new boyfriend would want to see her before leaving. Mike would call out her name.

But this intruder was noisily being as silent as he could.

Her bedroom door was still open like she'd left it, which made her assume no one had been into the bedroom yet.

She was about to go and peek out into the hallway when she heard another sound out somewhere in her house, and changed her mind. Instead, she looked across her bed for her cellphone. Discretion might be the better part of valor here. As in . . . *Lock the frigging bedroom door and call the cops. This intruder might have a gun.*

But her phone wasn't in the bedroom.

Damn it, it's outside in the living room with Mike's. And the cordless is on the kitchen counter.

There was no point in shouting for help. Her neighbors were too few and too distant and were probably still at work. And anyway, Brooke most definitely didn't want to lock herself away and hide. She wasn't a 'hidey' kind of person.

She glanced at her bedroom windows. She wasn't trapped in here. She could easily flee the house if she chose to, but she hated the thought of running away from her own home, even if it was necessary to do so to save her life. It was totally uncharacteristic for her to run from a fight of any kind. Her natural instinct was to stand and defend her turf.

It'll be good to go with my phone though, so I can call the police once I'm outside. I'll just have a peek out into the hallway, then I'll unlatch the window and be on my way.

She hurried over to the bedroom door and peeked out into the hallway. A man in black clothes and a ski mask was just stepping out of the bedroom down the hallway, the one closest to her living room. The intruder's body shape didn't immediately remind Brooke of anyone she knew, but she did instantly recall what Mike had told her about the driver of the car that had killed Bob—that the killer driver had been wearing a ski mask. So this must be he then.

This intruder was clearly here looking for her, but had not known where in the house she was, hence the noisy search.

Oh, so you're here to kill me too, she thought as a red rage filled her mind.

The man in the ski mask noticed her then and waved a long knife at her. "I'm gonna gut you with this knife, bitch!" he growled.

Brooke shook her head at the guy's nerve to break into her house and dare to threaten her. She forgot about fleeing through the bedroom window behind her. She saw no need to call the police either; she could handle this on her own.

The intruder was coming for her now, waving his knife at her. "I'll stab you, bitch!"

Oh, you dumbass, she thought. *You're so goddamn beaten up right now, you're gonna be spitting your teeth out and shitting blood!*

"Yaaaah!"she yelled and charged at him.

She covered more ground than he did in a shorter period of time and they met very near to the bedroom door he had just exited from.

He swung the knife at her, but she easily ducked away from the thrust. This guy was no trained fighter, that was certain. She hit him hard in the chest, taking satisfaction in the crunch of his bones as his ribs snapped and he howled in pain.

"Who is the bitch now, huh?"

Brooke was in the ascendancy now and she stalked him like a tigress as he dropped the knife and backed away from her out into her living room.

There he turned to run, but she, feeling the assured thrill of the kill, grabbed him and pulled him back, then spun him around and kneed him in the testicles.

He collapsed like a deflated balloon, lying on the ground at her feet, his hands clasped between his legs while he both groaned in agony and coughed up blood.

She knelt down beside him.

"Who are you, huh?" He was simply a pathetic wreck now, no longer any kind of a threat to her. She felt disgusted by her initial fear. Was this sniveling worm the reason why she had intended to flee her home?

"I asked you a question, bitch. Who are you? Talk or I will break your arm."

"Enough, enough! Please don't hit me again!" he gasped.

"So start talking, or I'll *really* hurt you."

Her quick success in subduing the intruder had however overridden her natural caution.

She reached out to pull off his ski mask, and next was completely taken off-guard when someone grabbed her hair from behind, yanked her head backwards and then hit her on the side of her head with something that fractured her consciousness.

Oh my God, there's two of them! she thought in surprise as her world instantly blurred.

Brooke didn't pass out. However, she immediately felt tranquilized. From her kneeling position, she slumped forward and then fell sideways. And as she hit the floor she suddenly noticed that there was a strange smell out here in her living room now, the smell of something rotten, the smell of decaying meat.

She lay motionless on the living room floor, fully conscious of the world around her, but too stunned to move her limbs.

A second ski-masked man now stepped around her prone body and helped the injured man on the floor back up to his feet.

And then, together, both men grabbed her by her feet and dragged her back into the hallway and then into her bedroom, where they stripped her naked and then tied her hands and feet to the corners of her bed.

Once this was done, the pair gagged Brooke with duct tape.

She lay there helpless, her mind boiling with angry thoughts: *Who are these two jerks, and what the hell do they want with me?*

Now she felt the beginnings of fear.

Neither of her attackers had said anything since dragging her in here, but now the shorter one, the one she had hurt, pulled out another large knife and advanced towards the bed waving it at her.

Brooke was certain she was about to be stabbed to death when she heard her front doorbell ring.

The man with the knife stopped and lowered it. He wiped blood from his mouth and then looked at his larger companion.

The buzzer sounded again. "Hey, Brooke, it's Mike. I'm back to pick up my phone."

"We'd better go and let him in," the taller man said to the shorter. "No point keeping loverboy waiting."

Brooke had no difficulty at all recognizing the speaker's voice. It was a voice she knew very well. But why? What the hell could possibly be *his* reason for doing this to her? To everyone?

"Yeah, we better go let him in," the shorter guy agreed, while coughing up blood over his lips. And once again Brooke was shocked. She recognized his voice too now. What the hell was going on here?

The ski-masked pair had already left her bedroom, however, and now Brooke could only hope that Mike would be able to escape from them and get help.

But that wasn't to be, as she heard a few seconds later.

"Hey, baby, it's me, Mike! Are you okay?"

No, I'm not fucking O.K., baby! she thought desperately.

She heard her front door click open, Mike's surprised voice asking, "Hey, who the hell are you?" and then there was the sickening sound of something hard striking something soft, and next the quiet and yet unmistakable thud of a body hitting the ground.

Oh, no, Brooke thought, as she heard the sound of her front door closing again. *Oh no!*

CHAPTER 31

Someone was slapping Mike in the face. "Hey, wake up, douchebag!"

Mike quickly came alive again. In the split second before he opened his eyes, an accelerated memory of what had happened flashed through his mind:

I returned to Brooke's house to pick up my cellphone, rung her doorbell a few times and then . . . a man in a ski mask opened the door and yanked me into the house and something hit me . . .

Shocked by his memories, he opened his eyes just as someone slapped him in the face again.

"It's okay, Eddie, he's awake now."

Eddie? What's he doing here? The slap had stunned Mike a bit, and he shook his head to clear it before focusing on his current situation.

The situation was dire: Mike now discovered that he was in Brooke's bedroom. Brooke was naked, gagged and tied spread-eagle to her bed. He, Mike, was also naked and gagged and was bound to an armless high-backed chair that must have come from Brooke's dining room.

Brooke was staring helplessly at him, wagging her head from side to side and making protesting sounds. Thankfully, she still looked unharmed. The bedroom drapes were all shut and the lights were on.

The two people who'd bound and tied he and his new girlfriend up were Kirk and Eddie Coombs, both of whom were dressed in black jackets and tees, black denim pants and black sneakers and who both also wore latex gloves. A black ski mask lay on the bed between Brooke's parted legs.

Eddie looked beaten up; his lips and chin were bloody and he was coughing painfully.

"Hmmph!" Mike protested against his gag. This made no sense to him. *Okay, so Brooke snubbed Kirk at the funeral, but so what? Raynham is full of girls dying to sleep with Kirk . . .*

145

However, Mike couldn't ponder on this. Eddie was pressing a sharp knife to his throat.

"Hmmmph!" Mike said, pulling his head as far back as he could to escape from the knife blade.

"Now, listen very closely, loverboy," Eddie said. "I know you've lots of questions you wanna ask me and Kirk, so I'm gonna pull off the duct tape from your mouth now. But if you dare make a single noise—if you dare try yelling for help—I'm gonna slice your dick off." He leaned forward and growled: "Do you understand?"

Mike quickly nodded.

"I ain't joking about cutting your dick off, Mikey, and then we'll kill Brooke too."

Mike nodded again and Eddie pulled the strip of silver tape away from his lips.

"Guys, what the hell are you two doing? What's the matter . . . what's . . . ?" Then the light of understanding flashed in his mind. "Oh shit—don't tell me you're the ones who've been . . ."

Eddie strode back over to Kirk's side and both brothers sat at the foot of Brooke's bed, concealing her from view.

"Guilty as charged, Mike," Kirk said. "Yeah, we're the one's who are killing everyone."

"That's right," Eddie sputtered and then winced in pain like his chest was really hurting.

Mike's bafflement at the siblings' admission was clearly etched on his face. "But . . . but . . . but . . . why?"

"Everything is entirely your fault, man," Kirk said. Mike now paid attention to Kirk's facial expression. Kirk's eyes showed no mirth, no remorse, and no mercy. He was smiling but somehow that smile managed to be angry at the same time. Kirk gestured back at the bound girl on the bed. "Everything that's happening now and that earlier happened is entirely your fault, Mike."

"Yes it is," Eddie agreed.

Kirk looks insane, Mike thought. Suddenly he had no doubt that Kirk and Eddie had killed both Ashley Hunt and Bob. But why had they done so?

"What do you mean, it's *my* fault?" he asked helplessly. "I didn't kill anyone."

Kirk laughed and got up. "Oh, but you're the one that introduced that bitch Mortika to me, aren't you?"

Mike thought he got it. "Man, don't you think you're overreacting a bit? Yeah, Eddie told me she gave you VD, but that's normal enough with the number of girls you pick up. All I'm sayi—"

"Shut up!" Kirk growled at him, while starting to unbuckle his belt. "You've no idea what the hell you're talking about. That bitch didn't just give me the clap or syph or even herpes." Kirk unzipped his jeans and pulled them down. "Look at what Mortika did to me. Look at my dick now!"

Mike looked and the more he looked the wider his eyes grew until he felt they'd fall out of his face.

Kirk's penis looked like a bunch of purple-brown twigs growing out from his crotch. And very withered twigs at that. Mike counted: there were four of these penile twigs—each of them about the thickness of a regular USB cable and they were each about six inches long with a fat bulb at their ends. Staring at them, he was also reminded of the long, projecting stigma and stamens of some flowers. Kirk's testicles were shrunken and black; they looked exactly like prunes.

Oh, frigging wow! Am I so damned glad I listened to Master Slim back then! Kirk's dick looks like something you plant in the earth. No way is that thing any use for having sex with!

Mike stopped gawping at Kirk's crotch and looked back up at his face. "Morti . . . Mortika . . . *Mortika* did *that* to you, man?"

Kirk made no attempt to pull up his pants. "Yes, she did, you sonofabitch. And according to Master Slim—you knew all about it."

Mike looked confused. "I don't follow you, man. How does Master Slim fit into this?"

Kirk looked too irate to reply, so Eddie spoke for him. "It's like this, you jerk: The day after Kirk fucked Mortika his dick began splitting up, like the way you peel a banana. Well, he showed it to me and it clearly wasn't anything like a normal STD, so I told him to call Mortika—who had by then left our house—and ask her what she had." Eddie paused to spit out some blood on the floor. "Okay, so he called her and the bitch claimed she didn't know anything about it . . . that maybe—"

Kirk took over the narrative again. "Mortika insisted that I'd picked it up from some other chick. Then she advised me to go visit Master Slim; said he'd be able to get rid of whatever it was I'd contracted. So

Eddie and I drove out to the old man's place . . ." Looking pained, Kirk fell silent.

"And he laughed at Kirk," Eddie said in a pissed off voice. "That old fool laughed at my brother. Said it was all Kirk's fault that he'd gotten burnt by Mortika."

Kirk smirked. "And, Mike, Master Slim also said he'd recently—just the previous day, in fact—advised a 'nice young man' to break up with Mortika . . ." He stepped closer to Mike, until his transformed crotch was just inches from Mike's face and Mike thought Kirk intended to rub his face in it. (Close up like this, the whole unnatural genital arrangement had an unpleasant odor, like corrupted incense.) But thankfully Kirk didn't touch him with it, he just bent over, grabbed Mike's head painfully by the hair and said, "Does that 'nice young man' description sound familiar to you? 'Cos it sure does to me. That 'nice young man' that Master Slim warned was clearly you."

"And then you brought her to our house," Eddie said. "On the pretext that you two were headed somewhere." Eddie laughed, though he clearly instantly regretted doing so and grabbed his chest in pain. "You know, I knew there was something really fishy about the way you seemed completely unconcerned when Kirk snatched Mortika away from you. Yeah, that night you almost seemed relieved that you'd gotten her off of your back."

Mike ignored Eddie. Yes, Eddie was telling the truth—he had been pleased to be free of Ashley Richard aka Mortika. But that still didn't fully explain their raging.

"But couldn't Master Slim just reverse what's wrong with your dick?" he asked Kirk, who was still painfully twisting his hair as if trying to rev up the headache Mike had revived with.

Kirk let go of Mike's hair and stepped away from him, much to Mike's relief as it took the guy's ghastly transformed crotch away from his face, along with its sickly incense-like smell.

Mike looked over at the tied-up Brooke. Brooke's eyes were goggling too. Kirk had turned towards her as he stepped away from Mike and she now had her first proper look at what their captor was pissed off about. Brooke looked utterly horrified by the revolting transformation of Kirk's penis into a bunch of withered twigs, with those prune-like balls.

Laughing bitterly, Kirk turned to look at Mike again. "No, dude, Master Slim *couldn't* fix it. He told me it was a magical curse, something that Mortika had brought upon herself while trying to hex a fellow witch who was stronger than her, and that I'd be stuck with it for the next seven years."

"Seven years? Oh, man, I'm so sorry to—"

"But all that time, he was laughing," Eddie said, "and I just knew he was lying. He just didn't want to help Kirk because he thought Kirk was promiscuous and needed to be taught a lesson."

"So Eddie and I both left," Kirk said. "But that night, we returned to his place at around midnight and killed him."

Mike felt a chill run through him at the admission of guilt. "You're the guys who killed the old occultist?"

Eddie nodded. "Oh, he wasn't alone—his son was there too, along with some other guy from out of state. But they were all drunk. So we killed them, chopped them up and made a mess of the place and made it look like someone had been performing satanic rituals in there." Eddie tapped his right temple with a finger. "We wore gloves of course . . ."

Mike sighed. "Where's Mortika?" He nodded towards Kirk's crotch, though it hurt him to look at that mess. "Guys, she's a witch. Even if the old guy wouldn't help Kirk, it shouldn't be too much for her to do so, since she was responsible in the first place."

Kirk shrugged. "Now why didn't *we* both think of that?" He gestured to Eddie. "Go fetch the witch."

Mike looked at him in surprise. "She's here?"

"Yeah, outside in the living room."

In the living room? Mike didn't like the sound of that, but Eddie was already leaving the bedroom. *Shit, is Mortika a part of all this killing too? Because now, Kirk and Eddie have already killed five people.*

Kirk spent the interim pulling up his pants, which gave Mike and Brooke relief from viewing his grossly mutated genitals.

Eddie was back less than a minute later. Mike heard his footsteps coming in through the bedroom door behind him and also caught a whiff of an unmistakable smell.

Oh, my dear Lord, what the . . . ?

The smell entering the bedroom with Eddie was the reek of a dead animal; one that had been dead for a while. The nauseous odor filled the air as if Brooke had hidden roadkill under her bed.

Eddie stepped into view holding a trash bag, which he now proceeded to open up.

"I guess I didn't explain myself too clearly," Kirk said, pointing towards Eddie. "Most of Mortika is currently in some trash bags that we're gonna leave in your house later tonight. But here's her head!"

Eddie pulled Mortika's rotting head out of the trash bag. The head swarmed with maggots. Mortika's eyes were open, though they'd lost their emerald luster now. Similarly her red hair had lost its shine. Her face was a tapestry of decay, a patchwork of rotting meat. Her grossly swollen tongue protruded from her mouth as if she'd either hung herself or had been strangled before her decapitation.

Brooke Lee had so far been looking tough and angry. She'd started squirming furiously on the bed when Eddie pulled Mortika's head out of the trash bag, but when Eddie grinned at her, knelt on the bed and placed the severed head next to her head, she immediately fainted.

"Hey, cut that out!" Mike said. "Stop that!"

Kirk nodded to Eddie. "Stop wasting time."

Eddie nodded back and shrugged. "Yeah, it's no fun now that she's fainted."

He got up, but left the severed head positioned between Brooke's knees. While looking at her in hatred, he clutched his chest and winced, then spat blood on her belly.

Mike felt a sudden fading of all hope. "Guys, you've murdered six people now. But I still don't get your reasoning. Kirk, okay, so Mortika fucked up your junk and *I* brought her to your house, but why kill everyone else?"

"It's all just to hurt *you*, Mike," Kirk said calmly, once more sitting at the foot of the bed. "See, once I realized that I was gonna be stuck like this—in this dickless condition—for a long while to come, with no pussy, I figured you didn't deserve to have any fun either. And so, Eddie and I decided to kill any girl you showed any interest in. That way, if *I* ain't getting laid, then *you* ain't either." He gestured back at the fainted girl. "So, it's goodbye to little Brooke here."

"You should've stuck to Brash," Eddie said. "Then we'd have left you alone, both 'cos those two bitches deserve some happiness in their pathetic lives, and also 'cos they'd be certain to make your life miserable with those tantrums they keep throwing."

"But no, you're too good for our family freaks, aren't you?" Kirk spat.

"You can't go on like this forever," Mike protested. "The cops are gonna catch you soon."

Eddie laughed and then spat blood. "Yeah, we already know that. An old flame of Kirk's at the Raynham PD keeps us up to speed on all the latest developments in the case. And so this is gonna be our last kill."

"It's clear cut and simple," Kirk explained, reaching back and patting Brooke's right leg. "We're gonna butcher her and frame you for the murder."

"The cops are gonna know I didn't do it," Mike said heatedly. "I'm not going to jail for you guys."

"*Dude*, who said anything about you going to jail?" Eddie mocked. "Once we kill Brooke, Mike, we're gonna smear you in her guts and then we'll lie you down on her body like you were raping her and then we're gonna kill you too. We got a gun here that we found in Master Slim's house—must've been his son Dave's. Anyway, we'll carry you over to Brooke's bed, get you nicely all smeared up in her body fluids, and then we'll shoot you in the head and place the gun in your hand. But first we'll paint some Satanist shit on the floor like we did at Master Slim's."

Kirk nodded. "A wonderfully neat murder-suicide for the cops to clean up. They'll assume you were so overwrought by Bob's death that you decided to take your own life."

"That still won't explain Bob's death," Mike said.

Kirk nodded again. "Yeah, true. But so what? Five out of six ain't bad. Even the cops gotta know that beggars can't be choosers. Law enforcement will simply assume you were lying all along and that Bob's death really was an accident."

Eddie nodded too. "You know, you've really got bad luck, Mikey. "We originally planned on just killing Brooke right now, and then doing you tonight once you got back home. We'd leave Mortika's corpse in your house along with some other evidence—the gun and some cocaine packages that we found at Master Slim's and smeared with his blood—but then you walked in on us now . . . so thanks, dude."

Kirk grinned and pulled a folded sheet of paper from a jacket pocket. "And just to help the cops see things our way, here's a suicide note written on your laptop and printed with your printer . . . explaining how and why you killed everyone . . ." He laughed at Mike's shock. "C'mon, man, what's so surprising? I used to be your housemate—I've still got the keys to the damn place. And you've told me your laptop password lots of times when I needed to use it."

Oh shit, I'm dead meat! Mike realized. He honestly saw no way out of this current predicament. Clearly he was about to die here and now. Both of the Coombs brothers had the same merciless expression on their faces.

And yes, the cops are certain to buy this whole murder-suicide frame-up thing, particularly once they leave Mortika's corpse in my house.

Mike glanced over at the rotting head lying between Brooke's legs. Brooke had revived from her faint and was weeping quietly, while gaping down at Mortika's decomposing head, the displaced maggots from which had begun crawling over her own legs. Other grubs, dislodged earlier when Eddie had laid the rotting head beside her own, crawled through Brooke's hair.

Dammit! Mike saw no point in their murdering Mortika, but then he saw no point in any of this madness.

And now of course, beheaded like she was, Mike had no way to prove Mortika's culpability in any of this. Yes, it was true that Master Slim had warned him away from her, but now that he thought back on his short relationship with her, he didn't recall the young Goth woman as being a naturally mean-spirited person. In fact, the second time that he had met her, and during the short period of their abortive romance, she had struck him as being genuinely interested in him, and not as someone with malicious intent who was merely looking for a victim to transfer a supernatural ailment to. Which might even mean that Mortika herself hadn't known that the spell she had cast on her rival witch had backfired and that she was now hexed. Or that, even assuming that she did know something about it (seeing as she had consulted with Master Slim; though Mike had no way of knowing if that was why she had visited the old warlock on the day he had first met her), she might not know the full extent of her spiritual sickness and the horrendous results it would produce in any young man she slept with.

And so, with Kirk, had Mortika (aka Ashley Richard) simply done what all the other young women in her shoes usually did? Had her fling with Kirk Coombs been merely an innocent seduction and nothing more?

Mike sighed. Now that she and the old man were both dead, there was no way to know the truth.

Yes, she had proved fickle, but he would be crazy to have wished her beheaded and butchered just because of that.

But Mike forced himself to put these grim reflections aside for the moment, because something here still bothered him. Something still didn't add up here.

"Eddie, I don't get what *your* investment is in this," he said. "Yeah, sure, Kirk's mad at me. I do understand that, but why are *you* aiding him?"

At that question, it was Eddie's turn to look too angry to speak.

"You don't get it, do you, asshole?" Kirk said. "My younger brother here was in love with Ashley Cummins, whom you drove to suicide by breaking her heart."

Mike looked over at Eddie. Eddie was blinking back tears from his eyes.

Mike quickly looked away again. *Oh no, not that again! Why the hell did Ashley have to fall in love with me and not with Eddie? They'd have been perfect for one another!*

"And so," Kirk went on, "Eddie is even more dedicated to ensuring that you suffer for what you've done than I am. He's one-hundred-percent committed to making you miserable." He smiled and gestured down at his crotch. "I'll supposedly be back to normal in a few years, while he . . ."

"*You* killed her, you sonofabitch!" Eddie suddenly growled in a voice quite unlike himself. "*You* drove her to kill herself!"

"In addition to which the kid is a true sociopath," Kirk said in amusement. "You should've seen the evil way he ran down Ashley Hunt that night. It impressed me no end. Honestly."

CHAPTER 32

Mike had no options to consider. He figured he could yell for help, but that would be certain to merely hasten his death, and besides, the street outside had seemed desolate on his arrival here.

But there has to be something I can still do. No matter how hard I try to escape from this, everything seems to endlessly revolve back to Ashley Cummins. It all revolves around Ash.

"Hey, Ashley Cummins!" he suddenly yelled. "How the fuck am I supposed to marry either a Brooke or an Ashley if these two assholes kill me here!?"

Kirk looked at him in surprise and then shook his head at Eddie. "He's starting to lose it."

"Answer me, Ash, goddammit!" Mike grumbled. "This is all your goddamn fault after all. If you hadn't killed yourself you'd have married Eddie and lived happily ever after. Give me a hint on how we're gonna escape from this mess!"

Eddie, more composed now after his own recent outburst of emotion, nodded back at Kirk and tapped his forehead with his index finger. "Yeah, he really is losing it."

"Better gag him again before a passerby comes to investigate the noise, or calls the cops"

"Hey, Ashley Cummins, you God-damned, evil, possessive, crazy, devil-worshipping bitch, answer me! Say something, God-da—"

Eddie slapped a strip of duct tape over Mike's mouth. "Shut up, man, you're giving me a headache!"

"Mmmph! Mmmph!" *Nah, it won't work,* Mike realized. *It takes a ritual to summon her, and both times I had to shed my blood to accomplish it.*

He hadn't really expected a response. He'd begun screaming for Ashley from sheer desperation, a drowning man clutching at the poisonous tentacles of a man-o-war jellyfish to save himself. And also out of anger for all this mess she had gotten him into.

But then he froze, because something unexpected *was* happening in the bedroom.

Over in the corner to the left of Brooke's bed, he could see a shape forming, a blurred shape like faded colors mingling in midair.

The shape was clearly the ghost of Ashley Cummins; Mike once more felt the same supernatural dread that had accompanied her arrival at Master Slim's place.

Oh yes, it most definitely was Ashley Brooke Cummins.

She was there, but not really there, like a stubborn smudge on a cellphone screen, or a fingerprint on a window pane that refused to be erased. He assumed that the depths of his desperation had proven a lure she couldn't refuse, and she had put herself to the effort of penetrating the barrier between Hell and Earth to see what the commotion was about. But now that she'd arrived in the human realm she was unable to solidify herself, unable to become more than just the suggestion of her own presence.

The irony of the situation wasn't lost on Mike: at the moment he, who had unwittingly summoned her back from her realm of darkness and torment to assist him, and who would gladly slice his arm open and give her all the blood that she needed to fix her form here, was both gagged and strapped down to a chair.

And I think that in these cases I have to offer my blood to her willingly as payment for her appearance. She can't just bite me like a vampire and drink as much as she likes.

After looking over at him and then realizing her impasse, Ashley seemed to reach a sort of compromise with herself. She did become properly visible to Mike, but then she faded out completely, and then she was there again for a few seconds. Then she faded again. And just as suddenly, after a short interval she was back in the room again. This time however, she didn't fade away. She was obviously remaining here solely by an effort of will.

She walked forward past the foot of the bed and stared down at Mike. Kirk and Eddie clearly couldn't see her. Nor could Brooke, who was still weeping while the maggots from Mortika's head crawled up and down her legs.

"No, Mike, I'm not going to help you out," the ghost of Ashley Cummins said. "Why should I? Your current crisis plays out perfectly for my benefit. After all, once Kirk and Eddie murder you now, you'll be here with me in the afterlife, and then we'll both be together forever." She waved smoke-like fingers at him. "Goodbye, honey pie. See you soonest."

But she didn't vanish yet.

Mike watched Kirk and Eddie . . . and Brooke. They clearly hadn't *heard* anything either.

Kirk was holding a knife that Mike instantly recognized as coming from a set of knives in his own kitchen; additional incriminating evidence.

"Hey, younger bro, how do we kill this bitch for best effect?" Kirk asked Eddie. "You know, so that the cops really think Mike freaked out and did a number on her?"

"Hmmm, lemme think a minute," Eddie said. "Let's . . ."

". . . Kill her like Ashley Cummins killed herself," the ghost said. "That way there's a clear link between her and another dead girl."

"Hmmm, that's a *great* idea," Kirk agreed.

Mike thought he understood what had just happened. Although neither brother had spoken, the ghost had implanted thoughts in both of their minds to the effect that they assumed they'd continued having their previous conversation in the silence.

"Yeah, that's exactly what we'll do," Eddie said, placing his hands on Brooke's belly and tracing an imaginary line from between her breasts down to her pubic hair. "We'll gut her and pull out her intestines."

"Yeah, bro, that's cool . . . draw a pentagram on the floor in her blood and place them inside it."

"We've just gotta ensure we get Mike's forearms really red—say up to the elbows. And lots of blood on his dick . . . some pussy secretion too."

"And remember not to step in the blood like you did last time. You almost gave us away."

"Yeah, yeah, whatever. Don't blow a goddam fuse over it."

Mike looked over at the ghost. She made a show of blowing him a kiss and then blurred and faded from view.

He turned back to staring at the bed. Having heard the fate intended for her, Brooke was once more fighting to get free. Mike began struggling too, but his hands were too tightly bound behind him.

"Sorry, Brookey, but it's time to say goodbye!"

Kirk blew her a kiss and then stabbed her in the belly.

CHAPTER 33

"Wow, honey, don't you just wish you agreed to date me now?" Kirk asked Brooke Lee as the blood welled out of her wound. "Sure, there ain't anything sexual I can do for you in my current state of dick,"—he jerked the bloody knife from her belly and pointed it at Mike—"but at least you wouldn't have embarrassed me in front of that piece of shit over there . . ."

Brooke was staring wide-eyed at him as he rammed the knife deep into her body again. The tape across her lips meant that she couldn't speak but her eyes screamed at him to stop killing her.

". . . And you'd still be alive, bitch. Now you're simply gonna be dead, and the dead are just statistics for the cops to compile."

"Hey, bro, gimme the knife. You're starting to lose it yourself."

Kirk grunted and handed Eddie the knife. Then he sat on the edge of the bed and watched Eddie work.

Mike had to agree that Eddie really was a Grade-A psychopath. As he sliced Brooke Lee open from chest to crotch, Eddie had a calm look on his face like he was only making sandwiches. His motions were precise and methodical.

Brooke was jerking and shuddering as more and more blood squirted out of her belly. And then suddenly, her body arched up from the bed. She hung stiff like that in midair for a moment, then slumped down dead. A thin dribble of blood seeped out from under the left edge of her tape gag.

Eddie smiled at Kirk and then began pulling Brooke's intestines out of her. He piled the slimy loops up on the bed beside her and then fiddled around inside her body, looking for where to cut them free of her. Brooke's belly yawned open like that of a gutted fish and her bed looked like a lake of blood. Eddie, remarkably, had very little blood on him. Kirk too was keeping out of the way of getting splattered.

They're both behaving as if they've murdered others in the past!

Mike was sweating bullets now. It was clearly almost time for him to die too.

"Okay, now we paint the pentagram on the floor." Kirk got up and opened up a leather satchel lying on Brooke's dressing table. From it he pulled out a small paintbrush.

Mike winced as Kirk dipped the brush into Brooke's corpse and stirred it around inside her. Eddie stepped out of the way to let Kirk past him. Kirk knelt beside Mike, and after giving him a chilling "You're next!" smile, began sketching a bloody witch's star on the bedroom's polished floor.

Mike was enraged by what was going on. He wished he wasn't gagged. He wanted to speak, to scream at these two mad people to stop. He wanted to leap out of the chair, yank the paintbrush from Kirk's hand and shove it down his throat till he choked on it. He wanted to throttle Eddie's scrawny neck, to choke him until blood squirted from his nostrils and eyes and ears. And he was certain that had he not been tied to the chair he'd have managed to accomplish both of these aims.

Oh . . . shit! I feel so goddamn useless now. Brooke trusted me and I . . . I've completely let her down.

Then he noticed that Eddie was looking at him with an evil smile on his face.

CHAPTER 34

Kirk had meanwhile used up all the blood the paintbrush had previously soaked up and had now returned to the corpse for more 'paint.'

"Hey, bro," Eddie jokingly asked his older brother while the latter swirled the paintbrush about in Brooke's belly, deeper this time, "Why do us guys have nipples? I mean it ain't like we're gonna be breastfeeding kids, right?"

Kirk paused in his gory task. "I dunno. Never considered it. Why you asking anyway?"

Eddie pointed his knife at Mike. "I'm just wondering what he'll look like without any . . . nipples, I mean."

Kirk laughed and pulled the blood-soaked paintbrush out of Brooke's corpse again. "Wow, you *are* sick! Go for it, man!"

No, no, no! Mike thought in increasing horror as Eddie approached him with the bloody knife and with a manic smile on his face. *No— don't!*

But Eddie did. With his lips stretched sideways in a wide grin, he pulled Mike's left nipple out from his chest.

Mike now silently prayed for Ashley Cummins's ghost to return already and mentally tell the brothers that she wanted him intact, nipples and all, in the afterlife, but it didn't happen. Ashley didn't show up again.

Eddie began slicing Mike's nipple off.

Mike flinched as if being electrocuted as the knife cut through his skin. Shit! There was pain and then there was *pain*. In a million years, he'd never have believed pain like this existed in the world. And Eddie was taking his time with the cutting, while all the while still grinning at Mike. Mike trembled and squirmed against the chair and tried not to weep and tried not to piss himself as the agony continued and blood squirted from his chest.

Finally the agony ended. Eddie had severed a large circle of skin that included Mike's left nipple. He scowled at it and then coughed painfully and spat bloody phlegm on the floor.

Kirk had finished painting his pentagram and was watching. "Yeah, I like," he nodded in approval as Eddie waved the bloody circle of flesh at him. "Do the other one too."

Nooooo! Mike tried to scream, but Eddie had already pulled out his right nipple also and begun slicing it off. The seemingly endless, sadistically-prolonged agony consumed Mike again. Once again he fought not to weep or to wet himself, but then wondered why, if the only reason he was doing so was to salvage his pride in front of these two madmen who were going to murder him anyway.

Eddie sliced the nipple all the way off, leaving Mike with two weeping red circles on his chest. He waved both severed nipples at Mike, asked, "How do you feel now?" and then covered Mike's eyes with the two patches of bloody skin. "Wow, dude, you've got nipple-eyes, the chicks are all gonna love you!"

Kirk's laughter filled the darkness Mike was experiencing with his eyes covered. "Okay, enough fun and games, let's get her intestines down here on the pentagram and him up on the bed so we can get the fuck out of here."

The pressure of wet flesh on Mike's eyes was removed and he opened them, causing his nipples to drop into his blood-splattered lap. Despite the raging pain across his chest now, he felt disgusted and horrified as he watched Kirk and Eddie scoop up Brooke's intestines.

Just as with everything else, including Eddie's mutilating him, the pair were taking care to avoid getting blood on themselves. This was of course impossible to completely achieve, but as far as Mike could see, both of them would be able to walk down the street without arousing any public suspicion after a simple cleanup with soap and water.

"Hey, what the hell is going on in here!?"

"Yeah, Eddie . . . Kirk, what the fuck are you two doing?"

The voices were so unexpected that Mike at first imagined that he'd imagined them, then he thought that Ashley Cummins's unhelpful ghost was back in the bedroom with them.

But then he realized that it was the Lawrence twins, Brash, who'd just burst into the bedroom. If previously he'd been trying not to wet himself from agony, now he almost wet himself from sheer relief.

Kirk and Eddie were clearly as surprised as he was; both were staring towards the bedroom door, through which Mike assumed the Siamese twins were having to navigate sideways.

But they apparently got it done very quickly, which was only to be expected considering how long they'd been stuck together and the amount of practice they must have had through the years of entering buildings not designed for the conjoined.

Within a few seconds, Brooke and Ashley Lawrence were standing on Mike's left and staring at their two cousins who were standing on Mike's right. The girls were still dressed in their 'secret agent' getup, but had removed the black sunglasses.

Mike's relief increased when he saw that both twins held revolvers in their hands which they were pointing at the brothers.

"What are you two freaks doing in here?" Kirk asked angrily.

"No," Brooke said in an admirably calm voice. "The real question is—what are *you* two sickos doing in here?" Brooke pointed her gun at the bed. "You fucking killed Brooke? Are you two nuts?"

"And . . . and . . . you cut Mike's tits off! Are you two crazy!"

"Keep your voices down, both of you!" Kirk snapped at the girls.

"Listen, it's not what you two think, okay?" Eddie said amiably then once more winced in pain.

Brooke smirked at him. "Oh, yeah? Alright, we're listening, Eddie. What is it then? You're just harvesting her organs for the Red Cross or to donate them to poor kids in third world countries, or what the fuck!?"

"Oh wow, this had better be good," Ashley agreed. "Your explanation for cutting off Mike's nipples had truly better be fantastic. I liked sucking on them."

"Me too!"

"Hey, hey, girls, it wasn't us who killed Brooke Lee," Kirk said. "It was Mike who did it. We just tied him up 'cos we didn't want him running away before the cops arrived."

"Yeah," Eddie agreed. "That's exactly what happened."

Brooke shook her head. "You two assholes are such bad liars that—"

Kirk charged at the twins then, but Mike, who had been watching him closely, stuck out his foot and tripped him up. Kirk went sprawling and hit the ground at the twins' feet, but he quickly rolled over again while the girls got out of his way.

In the meantime, however, Eddie had grabbed his knife up from the bed and was also lunging towards the girls while Kirk was holding onto Ashley's wrist and trying to disarm her. At least he was until Brooke stuck her gun in his left eye and pulled the trigger.

Bang! Kirk's brains burst out of the rear of his head and he slumped down to the floor, letting go of Ashley's arm.

Eddie had reached the twins, but then, seeing that Kirk was dead and Ashley was free to shoot again, instead of attacking them he instantly retreated, ducked behind Mike and placed his knife against Mike's neck.

"Drop your fucking guns or I'll slit his throat, you freaks."

"Don't call us freaks, Eddie! We're as normal as everyone else."

Eddie laughed loudly. "Yeah, whatever, like everyone else I know looks like they had an accident in a superglue factory." He straightened up and pressed the knife harder against Mike's throat, so that it broke the skin and drew blood.

"Hey, stop hurting him!" Ashley yelped.

"Yeah, yeah, I know you two bitches like him a lot. I can see it in your eyes. So put your guns down or I'll kill him. Do it! Right now or else—"

"Okay, okay! We will."

"Yeah, just don't hurt Mike!"

Mike looked at the twins' faces. Brooke looked pissed off, while Ashley looked miserable. Personally, he didn't want them to disarm themselves. With Kirk dead, Eddie was certain to pick up the twins' guns and shoot them both. And Mike wasn't about to let that happen to these two girls.

I failed Brooke; I won't fail the twins too.

The twins looked defeated and were already lowing their guns.

"Hmmph! Hmmph!" Mike grunted at them, shaking his head fiercely when they looked at him.

"I said drop the fucking guns or he gets it!" Eddie spat at the twins.

Then, throwing caution to the winds, Mike kicked up hard with his feet, so that his chair toppled over backwards. As he fell to the floor, he felt Eddie's other hand, which had been resting on his shoulder, slip away.

Then he hit the ground hard, leaving Eddie standing alone in the middle of the bedroom, looking confused. Mike hoped that the twins would take advantage of this distraction, and they did.

Bang! Bang! Bang! Bang! Bang! their revolvers barked as they filled Eddie with holes. He was blown back against the opposite wall, his legs skidding through the pile of Brooke Lee's intestines as he died. Blood squirted out of him.

Both twins were fantastic shots: there was very little of Eddie's head left as he slid down to the floor.

And then the girls were loosening the duct tape from Mike's mouth. Then they dropped their guns and heaved his chair upright again. The fall had stunned Mike a little, but the adrenalin surge created by the danger had taken the edge off the hurt of banging his head on the ground. He just felt relieved that the three of them were still alive.

"Oh my God, baby!" Brooke gasped. "I can't believe those two creeps did this to you!"

"Yeah, I'd never have believed that Eddie was as nuts as Kirk. I mean, I knew Kirk was a jerk and all—that's public knowledge—but we never suspected that he was really nuts."

Brooke kissed Mike on the lips and then grinned at him. "Hey, I'm sure you totally love us now, don't you, man?"

Ashley kissed him too. "Ah ha, see? We told you we were good for you and we'd be really good to you too. See? Without us you'd be dead now!"

"Girls," Mike gasped, "I do *totally* love you both now. I've never been more happy to see anyone before in my entire life."

"Too bad about your tits though, but maybe they can be reattached."

"Maybe, but even if they can't be, we love you all the same. You'll just be a little freakish like us."

"But we're not really freakish. We're nice, normal girls, just a little bit unusual, that's all."

"Don't worry about your nipples, baby. Guys don't need nipples anyway—you don't breastfeed."

"Yeah, we'll handle that for you."

The girls picked up Eddie's dropped knife and cut Mike free of the chair. He stood up. The twins hugged him, but had to let go because he howled out in pain when they pressed against his mutilated chest.

"Sorry, baby!" Brooke exclaimed.

"Yeah," Ashley agreed. "Those two bastards really did a number on you." She spat in the direction of Eddie's corpse.

"And they were gonna kill us too. I really can't believe we're family."

"They must've been adopted."

Mike was trapped in a whirlpool of conflicting emotions. Most prominent among these was the simple delight that he'd survived. He also felt an immense gratitude towards these two girls who'd rescued him, an all-consuming gratitude that threatened to become deep and intense love very soon; and he really didn't mind that at all.

But then he looked at the bed—at the mess that his two supposed friends had made of Brooke Lee—and an intense sadness filled him. While killing her they'd moved Mortika's head over to her left side. Brooke's death . . . Mortika's death—in fact, all of the deaths—were so needless, so meaningless, so evil. These murders were nothing but utterly pointless exhibitions of human cruelty. He glanced at Kirk's and Eddie's corpses and felt only revulsion and disgust. They'd both more than deserved what they'd gotten.

And now I need to call Detective Banks and let her know what's happened. Someone might have heard the gunshots and called the cops already, but . . .

But now Mike realized that even though matters had been resolved, something *still* didn't add up in all this:

"Hey, girls . . ."

For the moment Ashley and Brooke had turned away from him and were studying all the human wreckage in the bedroom with disgust.

"Brooke . . . Ashley . . ."

"Yes, baby?"

"Yes, honey?"

"I'm confused about something: how did you two know that I was here? Don't get me wrong—I'm delighted that you came and rescued me, but how did you know I was in Brooke's house?"

The normally bold pair now looked surprisingly bashful.

"Well, it's a little bit embarrassing to admit," Brooke said after a while, "but we've been following you around." She pointed to Brooke's gutted corpse. "We didn't really trust her after meeting her this morning."

Ashley nodded. "No, we didn't. We were sure she'd get you into trouble, so we decided to keep an eye on you both, just in case."

Mike nodded.

"We didn't want anything bad to happen to you," Brooke said. "That's why we followed you."

Mike nodded some more and managed to grin at the Siamese twins.

Ashley sighed. "Okay, okay, we've actually been stalking you. Our endless surveillance of you had romantic implications."

"But we didn't mean any harm by it," Brooke quickly added. "Hey, you're not angry with us, are you?"

Mike shook his head. "Angry? You're kidding, right? You girls have absolutely no idea how I feel about you both now."

He wondered how they'd realized he was in trouble. Had they peeked in the bedroom window, or what? And how had they gotten into the house afterwards? He'd not heard any sound of a forced door. Or had he missed hearing the sound while Eddie was mutilating him? No, he figured that one was easy to answer—Kirk and Eddie had broken into the house earlier, so one of its doors must have been left open.

"Oh, Brooke . . . Ashley . . . you two women are my favorite persons now," he said with deep enthusiasm.

But then his good mood changed: *Oh, heck, no!*

Ashley Cummins's ghost had just rematerialized in the same corner as previously. Just like before, she at first faded away a few times, but finally appeared to stabilize herself in the bedroom. Once she was fully 'here,' she smiled at Mike, formed the shape of a pistol with her thumb and first two fingers of her right hand, and placed it against her head.

She didn't say anything however. She just kept smiling at Mike.

The twins, of course, had no idea that there was another dead person—this one still alive—in the room with them.

"Oh, Mike, you've no idea how delighted I am that you're okay," Ashley said.

"Man, I'm even more delighted than she is."

"No, you're not."

"Yes, I am. Ash, you keep forgetting that Mike likes me more than he likes you."

"That's not true! Take that back right now!"

"Hell no, I won't!"

"Take it back, you bitch! You're lying, Mike likes me more than you."

"Does not!"

"Does!"

"Does not!"

"Oh, you nasty scheming bitch!"

"You're nothing but a conniving slut!"

"No, you're the slut!"

"No, you are!"

Mike was so shocked and disturbed by Ashley Cummins's return that it took him a while to realize that the twins had begun arguing about him again.

He tried to intercede: "Hey, girls, please be reasonable. I like you both equally."

But the twins weren't having it:

"Oh, shut up, Mike! Stop lying."

"Yeah, don't lie to us. Don't be silly. You can't love her, she's a tramp!"

"Yes, she is! You only like her to make me happy!"

"I don't know what you see in her!"

While talking, the twins had been making their way over to Brooke Lee's dressing table, and now they seated themselves facing it and resumed their argument:

"So what the hell is it with you anyway? Why's it that whenever a hot guy likes *me*, you assume it's *you* he's after?"

"You know, bitch, that's a great question! I've been wondering about that for the past twenty-three years that I've known you. Even when we were babies you had to have the breast with more milk."

"That's a damn lie. It's not my fault that momma had more milk on the right."

"Why the hell are you always so mean to me, huh?"

"Yeah, why are you so frigging mean? I'm your sister! Yeah, your sister!"

By this point, they'd both begun weeping copiously; the tears were streaming from their eyes.

As had happened the first time he'd experienced this weird display of irritation from the twins, Mike could only stare at them. *What? They're so wrapped up in their anger that they've completely forgotten they're in a room with four corpses and that we need to call the police? Yes, yes, yes, I do owe them both my life—it's a debt of gratitude I'll never get through paying, but . . . how . . . how in the hell am I going to be their boyfriend if they keep behaving like this?*

"You know, sometimes I think you just hate me!"

"Yeah, I do. I wish you'd just die!"

"See!? See!? I knew it—you want me to kill myself so that you can have Mike all to yourself. Oh, I wish I could kill you. You're just a selfish bitch."

"Look in the mirror, bitch; you're describing yourself—hahaha!"

There's really only one way to end this, Mike thought grimly. *If I kill myself here and now, then the twins won't have to keep arguing over me. I'll be dead and gone and free from them, and the next cute guy they meet will be their victim.*

He walked over to where their identical revolvers lay on the floor and picked both up. One of the guns felt heavier in his hand than the other and he figured that that one still had unfired ammo in it, so he placed it against his temple.

"Goodbye, girls. I'm gonna kill myself."

The twins didn't turn from staring at themselves in the mirror.

"See what you've done now! Mike's about to kill himself."

"Don't you dare blame me for that! It's your fault!"

"But, Brooke, we love him, don't we?"

"So don't be so selfish then!"

"Fuck you! You're the selfish one!"

"No, I'm not. Mike's killing himself because of you!"

"Meaning he loves me more, sis!"

"That is not what I meant!"

"But that's what *I* mean. You know what, sis? You're just jealous 'cos no one's ever killed themselves because of you! Hahaha!"

Mike shrugged. *Okay, it's time to leave the Lawrence twins behind. Life hasn't really treated me too well recently. All of these dead girls on my conscience, and now these two conjoined young women who are set on making my life a living hell. So much for equalizing the ratio of Brookes to Ashleys here on earth. I'd better just end it all here and now, and then maybe I can be happy with Ashley Cummins in the afterlife . . .*

It was the thought of Ashley Cummins that made Mike remember her and look in the corner to see if her ghost still lurked there.

She *was* still there in the corner, her mutilated body terrible and motionless. She was watching him while her lips moved silently as if she was praying under her breath. She was also obviously feeding on his despair as if it were her lifeblood; she seemed to be becoming more substantial by the moment.

The look on her face chilled Mike. She looked desperate and hungry. And it was now, as he watched the silent motion of her lips as her gaze seemed to be attempting to eat him up, that he realized what was happening to him:

She's messing with my mind! She's planting thoughts in my head just like she did earlier with Kirk and Eddie. Ash is lonely in the afterlife—in hell, or wherever she is—and so she's trying to make me commit suicide too, so that I'll be there with her for all eternity sharing her damnation!

The realization made him shudder. *Hell no, I don't wanna die. But . . . but . . .*

But 'Brash' had finished their argument. Next thing Mike knew, the twins were both hugging and kissing him again.

"Oh, we're so sorry, darling. Please put the gun down."

"Don't kill yourself. Don't be silly."

"Besides, if you commit suicide, we'll kill ourselves too, 'cos our lives won't be worth living without you."

"No, they won't."

"Oh, darling, please. We really do love you. We'll do anything—everything—to make you happy."

"We just got a little worked up and—"

"Yeah, that happens sometimes, it comes from the pressure of always being together."

With the muzzle of the gun still pressed to his temple, Mike asked: "How regularly do you girls get like this?"

Ashley giggled. "Hmmm, maybe once or twice a week. . . . But if either of us is having her period it might be daily."

"But we always get over it quickly," Brooke quickly added. "And . . . and once you know us better, you'll get used to it. You can just leave the house and go for a walk."

"Yeah, just put the damn gun down, Mike, before you shoot someone with it!"

"Yeah, baby. You know you don't wanna die. Who's gonna love you then!?"

"Yeah, you know you love us both too much for that!"

"Yes, you do love us two only, don't you? 'Cos there's no room for any other women in this relationship."

While the twins apologized and pampered him, Mike watched Ashley Cummins closely as he lowered the revolver from his forehead and dropped it on the bed.

The ghost at first looked frustrated when he dropped the gun, then she looked resigned to her defeat by the twins, then she looked really angry—and then she vanished.

The pressure on Mike's mind—the impulse to commit suicide—vanished when she did. He sighed with relief. He doubted he'd ever see Ashley Brooke Cummins again. And he had no plans of summoning her back to Earth either.

He managed to smile at the twins, who were once again hugging him—which felt like death because their extra-wide suit jacket was rubbing against the skinned areas of his chest again.

"Girls, call the police quick!" he gasped. "Ask for Detective Shania Banks."

Calling the police and explaining the ghoulish situation in the bedroom focused the twins' attention away from him for a while. Mike used that interlude to locate his pants and pull them on. His chest hurt too much to chance wearing his shirt. He located his removed nipples under the chair he'd been bound to and held on to them; hopefully *they could* be reattached.

Then he stood in the doorway and watched Brash—Brooke and Ashley Lawrence—the Siamese twins he'd just dedicated himself to.

"The cops are coming," Brooke said.

"Yeah, and they're sending a message to Detective Banks too."

Mike nodded. The twins were smiling at him, their white teeth light amidst the horrible darkness of murder and nastiness that filled the bedroom. And he'd just realized again that the girls made him really, really happy.

"Don't you ever fight over me again," he told them. "I love both of you equally."

They began giggling.

And as for living with them—being their boyfriend, loving them and coping with their occasional tantrums?

Mike knew that that was going to take some getting used to. But he intended to give it his best shot.

Mike Broadman figured he owned Brooke and Ashley Lawrence that much at least. They were really great young women and as such they deserved to have a boyfriend who really cared about them. Mike believed he was the one to fill that emotional space in their lives. So what if they were a little different from other people--from other young women? Their difference would hopefully help keep the relationship from ever going stale. Anyway, he was looking forward to spending his life with them. Really looking forward to facing the future with both of them by his side.

He crossed over to the twins and began kissing them and reassuring them of his love for them.

Brooke and Ashley Lawrence really appreciated that.

The End.

ABOUT THE AUTHOR

Wol-vriey is Nigerian, and quite tall.

He believes there actually are things that go bump in the night.

He writes horror fiction—for adults only, please. And also some surrealist stuff.

Wol-vriey blogs at: *http://oddityfarm.wordpress.com*

WOL-VRIEY
BIZARRO AND TRANSGRESSIVE FICTION

BOSTON POSH (BUD MALONE #1)

In 2028 AD, the USA is a nation ravaged by hungry dragons and dinosaurs. In Boston, Massachusetts, private eye Bud Malone is hired to rescue a kidnapped heiress. But nothing is as it seems.

Malone works to unravel a tangled web involving Boston Chinatown, a 200-year-old woman with a 9-year-old body, white robots, a human-liver-eating psychopath, a golem, a porcelain dragon, and a snake goddess with a crush on him. There's also a woman obsessed with chicken sex. Then Malone meets Posh Lane, a gorgeous call girl who's desperate to quit her pimp.

Romantic sparks ignite between Posh and Malone, but Posh's past suddenly catches up with her in a BIG way. To save Posh, Malone agrees to run a quest for Earth's new rulers, the Forks. But, Malone has no idea that agreeing to the Fork's odd request will send him on the weirdest trip he's ever been on in his life.

BOSTON CORPSE (BUD MALONE #2)

MAGIC CAN BE MURDER! - Drag queen Lucy Tang is back in Boston, and is hell-bent on settling her vindetta against casino owner Sookie Ling. And suddenly, Bud Malone, PI, has the case of his life to resolve.

When Boston's robot police force are baffled by a mind transfer case, they come to Malone for help. The one person who can likely help Malone out here is the witch Soledad Bathory. But Soledad seems to know a lot more than she's telling him. It's a case not made easier when Malone meets Soledad's beautiful cousin, Josephine 'Slave' Bailey. Slave has her own plans for Malone, most of which involve teaching him BDSM and making him her new Master.

Oh, and Rick Rogers owes Sookie Ling a whole lot of money, a gambling debt that's going to be literally Hell to pay!

BOSTON CORPSE - Not your average detective novel!

Burning Bulb

WOL-VRIEY
BIZARRO AND TRANSGRESSIVE FICTION

BOSTON LUST (BUD MALONE #3)
"Bless it, Father, for she has sinned."

Seven murdered gay women, all their bodies completely drained of blood. All also with large parts of their bodies dissolved away like acid has been pumped into their veins.

Bud Malone has to find the female vampire preying on Boston's lesbian population.

Then Malone meets the beautiful Trudi Carmen and the case gets even more tangled. Trudi needs Malone's help in recovering a ring that's gone missing. But how in the world is one little black ring related to either the dead women or their killer?

Resolving this case will lead Malone deep into Lucy Tang's legacy –The Abstracta. And then to the city of Genesis.

Boston Lust –Just when you thought Bean Town was safe to visit again.

HELL DANCER

Six people find themselves trapped in Detention, a nightmare realm where the demonic Schoolmaster is hell-bent on reforming them . . . until they die.

Porn superstar Venus Deluxe came to Springfield, MA to party, and next found her life hanging by a thread. One wrong answer will mean her death.

Suspended BPD detective Tanya Rockford was trying to stop one kind of violence, but found a terrifying another. With her and her companion's lives hanging in the balance, it's going to take all of her courage and resourcefulness to escape this hell she's stumbled into.

Porn stud Chad Cannon has made a career from his ten-inch penis. Here in Detention, however, it's his brains that matter. He'll soon be hoping all the pot he's smoked over the years hasn't completely messed up his memory.

The three students, Sherri, Jordan, and Mike? They were all just in the wrong place at the right time. Will anyone survive Detention? The evil Schoolmaster doesn't plan on letting that happen . . . .

Burning Bulb

WOL-VRIEY
BIZARRO AND TRANSGRESSIVE FICTION

VAGINA MUNDI

Rachel Risk is a professional thief with super-strong hair that can stretch like tentacles to manipulate objects. Ashley Status has both a digitally augmented brain, and 'muscle-purses' in her arms and legs in which she stores inflatable objects—cars, guns, rocket launchers, etc.

When Raye is framed as the fall girl in a jewel robbery, the pair flee Chicago's vengeful robot gangsters and take refuge in the Hotel Bizarre, where the gorgeous 'vagina singer,' Femina, is performing for a week.

But the Hotel Bizarre is even stranger than its name suggests, and very soon Raye and Ash are involved in an deadly adventure, a struggle for survival the likes of which they'd never imagined possible with loads of deviant sex, drugs, music, and violence at every turn. And just what is the old woman in the skin desert really doing with all those cats glued to her walls?

VAGINA MUNDI—a Bizarro Hymn in praise of WOMAN!

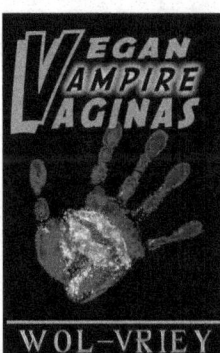

VEGAN VAMPIRE VAGINAS

The biggest bank heist in US history. And Tom Palmer can't remember pulling it off. And no, this isn't your standard case of amnesia. After a one-night-stand gone horribly wrong, Boston salesman Tom Palmer wakes up with a vagina implanted in his left hand. Then his day gets worse.

Tom is transported across space-time to a nightmare version of Boston, one where the Bizarro virus has transformed half the population into cannibals. Worst of all, Tom discovers that in this new Boston, he's the infamous gangster Pussypalm, wanted for robbing the Federal Reserve Bank of Boston a year ago. He also learns that the vagina in his hand is prophetic, i.e. it talks . . . after sex.

With 130 people left dead during his bank heist and six billion dollars missing, Tom knows he's living on borrowed time. It is in his best interests not to remember anything. Because once he does . .

Burning Bulb

WOL-VRIEY
BIZARRO AND TRANSGRESSIVE FICTION

VEGAN ZOMBIE APOCALYPSE

In the post-apocalypse worlderness, zombies rule the earth. They're allergic to meat, and brains literally make them explode. Zombies now eat blood potatoes, parasitic tubers grown in the flesh of humancows corralled in maximum security farms. Two fugitives meet in the ancient ruins of Texas. The first is Soil 15-f, a womancow who's escaped her farm a week before she's due to be killed and her blood potato crop harvested. The second fugitive is Able Kane, former head necros food technician, now sentenced to death for heresy. But Soil is no ordinary humancow.

Unknown to herself, she's the vegan zombie agricultural revolution, and the zombies desperately want her back. And the necros equally desperately want Able Kane dead. He's fled with a forbidden discovery which will reshape the world for the worse if used. And Able is just hardheaded/misguided enough to use it.

MELANIE NEMESIS CATCHPOLE

In Springfield, Massachusetts, Melanie Catchpole is hired to fetch back a magic teddy bear worth millions of dollars from a warehouse across town. Problem is, the warehouse is down in Springfield's O-Zone that totally weird sector of the city where Bizarro fell to Earth. The 'O' is a fairytale land, a place where dreams and nightmares literally live and breathe..

Worse still, the gingers—mutant cannibals—prowl the O. The gingers have already eaten everyone else Melanie's employers sent to get back the magic teddy bear.

Accompanied by the handsome but ruthless Doug Fisher (who she finds sexy but doesn't dare entrust her heart to), Melanie enters the O-Zone. Melanie and Doug are instantly caught up in an adventure they'd never have believed credible even if written as fiction . . . and Melanie's used to experiencing the very weird as the norm.

And now, additionally, there's a mystery to unravel: What does the dark, freezing-cold being called The Fixer want with Mary, the barkeep's daughter?

Burning Bulb

WOL-VRIEY
BIZARRO AND TRANSGRESSIVE FICTION

BIG TROUBLE IN LITTLE ASS

From Bizarro master storyteller Wol-vriey comes a truly weird western tale that will leave you awe-struck and on the edge of your seat...

In the town named Little Ass, tight-assed prostitute Rosa overhears a gunslinger's plans to assassinate rancher Edison Bennett. Once the badass Bennett learns of the plot, he ensures there'll be hell to pay for any attempt on his life!

Yes, it's going to take all of gunslinger Jude's shooting prowess, his eclectic collection of strange firearms, a trusty horse that requires an owners' manual, and the help of the lovely and invigorating Nell (who's EXTREMELY odd when the going gets weird), to survive the Bizarro hell that Edison Bennett unleashes in order to hold onto the land that he'd stolen from Madam Zizi.

BIZARRO 101 (A BASIC PRIMER)

Welcome to the strange place:

A collection of 37 flash fiction stories designed to introduce one to the Bizarro/New Weird Genre.

Weird, dreamy, nightmarish, absurd, sad, surreal, humorous . . . this collection of tales is all this and more.

***

"This primer is the very essence of any and all styles and types of Bizarro writing. Wol-vriey collects, distills, and bottles up these 37 tiny stories for your sensory enjoyment. This is an absolute must-read for anyone new to the genre, because it demonstrates the scope of what Bizarro is, and what it can be."
—Teresa Pollack, Bizarro commentator and blogger

Burning Bulb

WOL-VRIEY
BIZARRO AND TRANSGRESSIVE FICTION

Dr. Orgasm

Courtney Taylor is young, intelligent, beautiful, and successful. She also has a boyfriend who loves her deeply. The problem is, no matter what Courtney does, she can't climax during sex.

When Florence Rigid's communist forces destroy the city of Metaphor, Courtney and her friends Teresa, Highball, Miki, and Heather are cast into the midst of a quest to find the only person able to save the land of Innuendo—Dr. Carol Orgasm, wanted by the communists for developing the O-Pill, a wonder drug that grants women sexual ecstasy on demand.

The communists will do anything to get their hands on the O-Pill and prevent its reaching the millions of Innuendo's women. But Courtney desperately wants that pill too. And so it's now a race between Courtney and the communists to find Dr. Orgasm first.

And Courtney has no choice but to win this race. She must win it: For her own orgasm . . . and for the freedom of female sexuality everywhere.

PUSSY TRANSMISSION

Pussy Transmission were the most decadent Pop Art ensemble of the 90's. Led by the beautiful painter Isis Lynch, the trio revolutionized the art world. Then suddenly, without explanation, Pussy Transmission vanished into historical obscurity. Now, twenty years later, three women come to Lynch Place. Lily and Nina are journalists desperate to interview Isis Lynch. Raven, on the other hand, wants to find her boyfriend, who's gone missing inside Isis's house. Raven's worried—she's heard that Pussy Transmission broke up because Isis began dabbling in black magic . . . with devastating results. All three women will shortly wish they'd never left home. Particularly once the rats in Lynch Place start warning them that they're going to die . . . and Raven meets Betty Butcher, the bouncy supernatural psycho who's intent on chopping her into bits. Pussy Transmission, Baby! Just because . . .

Burning Bulb

WOL-VRIEY
BIZARRO AND TRANSGRESSIVE FICTION

GIRLS ARE NOT SMILING
Welcome To The Road Trip From Hell

Pagan is demon-possessed.

Lori is suicidal.

Britt is just terminally pissed off.

Meet three young Boston women on the run from the law, each with problems that will fuse into more than the sum of their individual parts, becoming a holocaust of sex and violence and terror, a literal rain of blood and horror and gore and evil.

And if that wasn't already bad enough, Pagan's pet demon is slowly transforming her into something both unspeakable and unholy. Truly, these girls aren't smiling.

BLUE NIGHTMARES
Consummate EVIL is coming.   It is relentless and unavoidable. It is Blue.

Jessica Schreiber is seeing things.   Very horrible things. Since arriving in Raynham for what should have been a relaxing vacation, she's been seeing *The Big Blue*.

Jessica is smelling things too—dead and rotting things that she can't see.   She is sure those dead and rotting things are dead people.   Lots of dead people.

Jessica's worst nightmares will soon become her reality.   Her reality will soon become a terrifying nightmare.

The tentacled residents of the House of Death have a lot that they wish to show Jessica Schreiber. They have a lot that they wish to tell her. But will she survive long enough to learn their lessons?

Burning Bulb
PUBLISHING

WOL-VRIEY
BIZARRO AND TRANSGRESSIVE FICTION

BRAINCHEW

It was supposed to be a simple jewel heist, but it went badly wrong. Chuck got shot and died.

Lance hid his friend's corpse in the Pleasant Street Cemetery. But that was a big mistake—there was something undead, something extremely hungry . . . something eXXXtremely horrible, buried in the Pleasant Street Cemetery.

And Lance had just woken it up.

They called the monster Brainchew because it ate brains. Human brains. And it preferred those brains fresh from the heads . . . of the living.

And now it was awake again, Brainchew planned on feeding big-time tonight. Oh hell yes, it did.

BRAINCHEW 2: OUT OF THEIR HEADS

After Tiff Hooper recognizes Josh Penham, the man who abducted her and kept her in his basement and abused her, she brings her three friends to Raynham for a night of well-deserved revenge on him.

Only things don't go according to plan.

It is never a good idea to leave a corpse in Raynham's Pleasant Street Cemetery. You run the very real risk of awakening what lies underground there. And that thing—Brainchew—is more horrible and more evil than anything the average mind conceives of even in its worst nightmares.

Brainchew is back! And this time the monster is extra-hungry. But there are plenty of delicious human brains about tonight, and Brainchew intends to eat them all before dawn.

Burning Bulb

WOL-VRIEY
BIZARRO AND TRANSGRESSIVE FICTION

DARIA: AN EROTIC NIGHTMARE

Even the best laid women can go wrong.

Daria Simpson is HUNGRY. She's HUNGRY for sex and bloodshed and death.

Shelly Parker just wanted to have a threesome with her boyfriend Craig and her best friend Erica. Everything was shaping up nicely for their weekend of sexual fun and games, until they stopped at the creepy Crossway Diner and met Daria.

From the moment they met Daria, EVERYTHING went wrong for them; and it went wrong in the most horrific and terrifying of ways!

Daria: Paranormal service has been resumed.

WET BONES

Greg is about learning the hard way that you don't mess with Aunt Grace.

Nine completely fleshless skeletons recovered in the Massachusetts woods. Two detectives on the trail of a horrible, hungry monster.

Broken-hearted Allie Jackson has a date with a creature from Hell.

Things are about to get well out of hand for everyone, and in horrifying, terrifying ways they don't expect.

Burning Bulb
PUBLISHING

WOL-VRIEY
BIZARRO AND TRANSGRESSIVE FICTION

MR. UGLY

When a rotting corpse appears and starts butchering Raynham's youths, there's really only one question that needs answering:

Is this faceless and rotting monster Peter Howard, or isn't it?

Problem is, Peter Howard died 15 years ago. So how can he possibly be back from the dead and murdering people with such relentless and incredible brutality?

Peter's mother Malicia, who's just been released from the lunatic asylum may have the answers to the crazy puzzle, but the two detectives investigating the deaths don't even know the right questions to ask her yet.

BRUTAL

Jane Winters is 28 years old.

She works as a checkout cashier in a department store. She's an attractive woman with a winning personality. She has both a photographic memory and an I.Q. of 189.

She's met the man of her dreams.

But she's also a cannibal with a unique and very scary mode of operation.

The group known as TULIP (The Urban Legend Investigation People) are out to either prove or disprove the legend of Insane Jane.

But have TULIP bitten off more than they can chew?

Burning Bulb
PUBLISHING

WOL-VRIEY
BIZARRO AND TRANSGRESSIVE FICTION

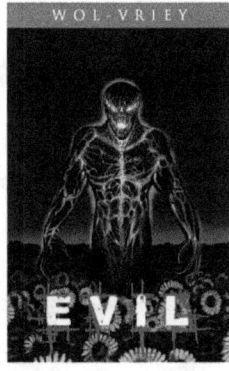

EVIL

The Evil began the week before Sylvia Stewart's 30th birthday.

Cathy Higgins died.

The Bargainer resurrected Cathy . . . for a price.

The price? Cathy's father Ronan had to plant some seeds for him.

But these were no ordinary seeds the Bargainer gave to Ronan Higgins. These were seeds from Hell: seeds which required human flesh as both soil and fertilizer.

And meanwhile, the unsuspecting Sylvia Stewart went ahead with the plans for her birthday party, which was to be held on Ronan Higgins' sunflower farm . . .

666

Ohio's State Route 666 stretches 14.7 miles between Zanesville and Dresden.

Most days, it's just a normal road with a funny name.

But for six minutes on the 6th of June each year, Route 666 becomes a gateway to somewhere else . . . a gateway to Hell.

Each year 13 unfortunates get trapped in the 666 underworld, with no way to get back home.

This year though, things are going to be very different. For one thing, there are currently a whole lot of turbulent human emotions at play in the underworld. And also . . . the psycho Al Gore is just about completing his collection of human heads.

And . . . what the hell is a church doing in Hell, of all places?

Burning Bulb

WOL-VRIEY
BIZARRO AND TRANSGRESSIVE FICTION

THE CLEAVERMAN

It began as a joke, a gag to pass the time that turned deadly. One rainy August night in Raynham, MA, nine friends jokingly invoke the evil phantom butcher called the Cleaverman.

These nine friends get a whole lot more than they ever bargained for. Because there's only one way to return the deadly Cleaverman back to the darkness he came from, and that is to solve his riddle, which starts: "Tell me the name of John Cleaverman's wife . . ."

And human beings being what we are, even with the Cleaverman out to butcher them all, our nine friends still manage to stir A WHOLE LOT of human misbehavior into the deadly mix.

At the rate they're going, it'll be a wonder if anyone survives THE CLEAVERMAN at all.

PERVERSE

When 21-year-old Heather Forrest accompanies three of her friends on a weekend trip up to Vermont, she has no idea what she's getting into.

Because, during a brief stop in the western Massachusetts woods, the girls get kidnapped and things go rapidly downhill from there. Soon Heather and her friends are fighting for their lives, fighting to survive the most perverted and impossible situation imaginable. And meanwhile, Hank Rollins is also in the woods, hunting the unholy monster that killed his wife and son . . . and he's hunting it with live human bait.

Oh yes, there will be blood. And there will be terror and buckets of gore also. And truly horrible atrocities will happen. Most definitely so.

Burning Bulb

WOL-VRIEY
BIZARRO AND TRANSGRESSIVE FICTION

THE VIRGIN

10 million dollars in prize money. 1000+ video cameras, lots of deadly weapons, 10 Suitors, 5 Virgins & 3 Hours . . . to keep your hymen intact.

Hailey Osborne wants to sell her virginity for a hundred thousand dollars. But then she's made an offer she really can't refuse: how about competing to win ten million dollars in a no-holds-barred underground game show, where all she has to do is remain a virgin?

There's just two problems:
1. Four other women also want that prize money.
2. There's ten suitors all contesting to take Hailey and the other virgins' precious hymens . . . by any means necessary . . .

But hey, it's just for 3 hours, right? How hard can it possibly be ? Hailey Osborne is about to find out.

THE BOOK OF ATROCITIES

Bestselling author Drake Melville has been missing for three years now. Drake vanished after publishing The Bleeding Oysters, an epic novel that set new standards for depictions of sleaze and depravity and human monstrosity in popular fiction. On vanishing, however, Drake Melville left a message for everyone, saying he'd 'left town' to go work on his follow-up novel The Book of Atrocities. The problem was, no one could find Drake. It seemed like he'd vanished off the face of the Earth. And now, three years later, Drake has just sent messages to his ex-wife Liz, his current (and abandoned) wife Melody; and his younger sister Chloe . . . asking them to meet him in Raynham, MA. Drake says he's now completed The Book of Atrocities and is ready to present it to the world. But there's a whole lot that Liz, Melody, and Chloe Melville don't know about Drake's Book of Atrocities. And unfortunately they're on their way to find out those excruciatingly painful truths. Because, see, Drake Melville is a VERY EVIL man with a VERY EVIL plan . . .

Burning Bulb
PUBLISHING

WOL-VRIEY
BIZARRO AND TRANSGRESSIVE FICTION

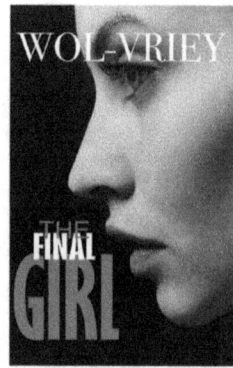

THE FINAL GIRL

Here there be monsters . . . because we made them.

At a secret location, 8 young women assemble to compete on the ultimate reality/game show—The Final Girl. The 8 contestants are: A young wife and her grown-up stepdaughter, a police detective, a prostitute, a nurse, a school teacher, and unemployed twin sisters.

The Final Girl is a no-holds-barred show beamed to an audience on the Dark Web, a show where murder is permitted and mutilation is encouraged.

The Rules:
1. Avoid being killed and eaten by the show's monsters and bogeymen.
2. Find the prize money—24 million dollars in cash.
3. Hold on to the money.

But only 1 woman can win. And to win The Final Girl reality show, that woman will need to be even more bloodthirsty and ruthless than the show's monsters.

Have a seat, everyone. The most dangerous game is about to begin!

WOMEN

John Miller must die . . . TONIGHT!

Megan Kemp initially went to the Penderson Mansion to collect a debt. But from the moment she stepped in there, getting back outside proved extremely difficult. And then what had merely been difficult for Megan suddenly turned deadly. Because something was going on in the Penderson Mansion that night. Five VERY ANGRY women had a score to settle, and no obstacle on earth would stop them. . . . And no one would get in their way and live to tell the tale either. "John Miller must die," the women had decreed, and it looked like the forces of Hell would help them accomplish their deadly aim tonight.

But as the night progressed, Megan, who was now trapped in a deadly game of cat and mouse in the Penderson Mansion, found that despite her own troubles, her biggest question was: "What the hell did John Miller do to anger these five women this much?"

Beware, folks . . . sometimes things really do go too far!

Burning Bulb

www.ingramcontent.com/pod-product-compliance
Lightning Source LLC
Chambersburg PA
CBHW070023260626
47159CB00005B/1929